PADDY MADIGAN
An Irish Idyll

Also by Herbert A. Kenny

Newspaper Row: Journalism in the Pre-Television Era
Israel and the Arts
Literary Dublin: A History
Cape Ann/Cape America
The Secret of the Rocks: The Boris Photographs
New England in Focus: The Arthur Griffin Story
(with Damon Reed)
Chess Trivia (with Peter Hotton)
A Catholic Quiz Book (with G. P. Keane)

Translation
The Divine Comedy (on tape)

For Younger Readers
Dear Dolphin
Alistare Owl

Poetry
Twelve Birds
Suburban Man
Sonnets to the Virgin Mary
A Boston Picture Book (with Barbara Westman)

PADDY MADIGAN
An Irish Idyll

A Novel by
HERBERT A. KENNY

THE IPSWICH PRESS
Ipswich, Massachusetts 01938

Acknowledgements

The author wishes to record his special indebtedness to his friends Thomas Halsted, Vas Vrettos and Neil Whitehouse; to his daughters, Ann Gonzalez and Susan Carroll; and to his publisher, Charles Getchell.

Cover photographs by Vas Vrettos. *(Front)* Irish island. *(Back)* The author near the grave site of his grandfather in Glasnevin Cemetery, Dublin.

ISBN 0-938864-24-6

Manufactured in the United States of America by Thomson-Shore, Inc., Dexter, MI 48130.

Published by
THE IPSWICH PRESS
Box 291, Ipswich, MA 01938

Dedication

To my wife, Teresa, and to our friend Dermot Kinlen, of Dublin, Ireland, whose hospitality is at the heart of this book.

Glossary notes:

Gardaí: Irish Republic police. Singular: garda.
Boreen: a small lane or roadway.

1

HE STOOD WITH his cap in his hand, very conscious of the mud on his wellingtons because she had suddenly looked down at them as if they smelled. She stood with her hand on the key in the door, her school books under her arm, looking directly at him so that he dropped his eyes. He was embarrassed because he had startled her, coming at her as he had so suddenly. He had waited half an hour for her to come along, and, wearying of his vigil, he had stepped to the alley beside her house to gaze down at the turbulent river, brown and swollen from the continuing rain, its banks green and the rushes glistening. Swans and a cygnet huddled on the shore. It was at that very moment that she had come hurrying along to the door of her house. Seeing her figure passing, he had dashed back to the street and had, breathing hard and flustered, come up to her, almost bumping into her, and had observed her jump in alarm.

"I didn't see you there," she said. They were the first words she had ever spoken to him. Despite the rain, he had taken off his cap and looked at her quite steadily but the awkwardness of the meeting drove from his mind the words he had rehearsed. He tried to recall them but his memory failed and the frank questioning stare of her blue eyes left him unsettled. She was hatless and the rain which had fallen on her hair was running down her forehead and her obvious discomfort disturbed him. He hastened to speak: "Could I walk you to the pub some night?"

He immediately felt like a fool. He wasn't even sure that she knew his name, however often she might have seen him walking back and forth before her house on his way in and out of the village. He had watched her on the street and in the shops and had tried to sit near her in church so that she might see him and he watched her, always hoping that she might speak to him. Several times their eyes had seemed to meet and he had smiled but then quickly hung his head when she had not smiled in return. On other occasions he had waited around the bridge pretending to be watching the water, but actually watching to gauge when she would come home from the training college, not on the bus usually but in the Ford sedan driven by one of the professors who lived in the town, a man too old to be considered a suitor. He even worked to adjust his schedule on the farm so that he might be in town when she did arrive in the afternoon.

This day he had driven the cows behind the barbed wire and walked to the main road to hitch a ride. He would have walked all the way but he welcomed the ride because he had started out forgetfully in his wellingtons, and realized he should have changed to his boots. He hesitated to go back and set his mother questioning him. There was, of course, no bus and he had no bicycle but was saving to buy one. Because of the ride, he had arrived more than half an hour beforehand, and she arrived earlier than usual, earlier than he had expected; so that, vigilant though he had been, he had botched his timing and forgotten the speech he had rehearsed. Now he stood in the rain, cap in hand, with his foolish question ricocheting around in his skull.

"Could I walk you to the pub some night?"

He was close to tears. She opened the door so hurriedly and so determinedly that he was afraid she wasn't even going to answer him.

"I don't go to the pub any more." The answer seemed as strange to him as his question but yet came as a relief or a release. He would not have been surprised by a blunt refusal such as always seemed to come to him. The gentleness of her voice, so different from the rasp of his mother's, gave him courage to speak again.

"I'm Paddy Madigan."

She stared at him and merely nodded. He felt she was expecting him to continue, to speak again, to add some sense to his remark, as if she saw her first refusal had not been sufficient to turn him away. He saw the slight motion of her head sending rain drops from her hair down over her high white forehead, and he was very conscious of her large blue eyes. He understood the banality of his second remark, and her reaction to it all, and paused, dreading to ask again, afraid not to, and sensing that he shouldn't have asked in the first place. He had no right to start what he couldn't finish. He owned nothing; he knew nothing. He should never have left school. He was the very type who needed it; and yet, after his mother took him out he was too embarrassed to go back. He had few books; he had no prospects where learning was concerned or where skills were needed. He was embarrassed at not even owning a bicycle, at his age, and if she had gone to the pub with him, the money would have had to come out of his bicycle savings.

"Couldn't we go some night to the music?"

His voice was hoarse and having spoken in a rush he now coughed. She had taken the key from the door and stood resolutely behind it, holding it half closed. He turned his head aside when he coughed and dropped his eyes. He raised them now pleadingly to her. She looked directly into his eyes and spoke again in her soft voice but with great firmness. "No, Paddy," she said, "I can't go out with you." He caught just the slightest emphasis on the last word, but knew that he was more likely to find it there than she was to put it, and she did add a phrase that eased his anguish. "I have to study."

"Yes," he said, fumbling with his cap. "Yes. Thank you. Very much, I mean." She closed the door and he stood in the rain, his cap still in his hand, until he looked down at it and, almost surprised to find it there, put it on with a jerk of his arm. He turned away and walked dejectedly toward the center of the village. Hardly conscious of the rain, he stopped at the bridge to watch the tumescent waters boiling over the spine of rocks in the middle of the stream. The turbulence of the waters matched something inside him and he thought of himself as the river tormented by the spine of rocks. Even as he leaned on the wet stone wall, the rain stopped. Two automobiles sped over the bridge, splashing water on him from a muddy puddle. He had to be home before the dinner hour to bring up well water for the cooking and the tea.

Looking up he saw old Dennis Wogan move across the street into the square toward the Long Bar as he had every day for seventy years, it seemed. Dennis was close to ninety and had never married. Paddy walked in the same direction, waited until Dennis had gone into the pub, and then followed.

The afternoon's overcast had made the day dark indeed, but the interior of the pub was darker still and he could not see at first who was there. Behind the bar in a dim light, Mrs. Fleming stood, wizened and unsmiling, her black lacquered hair like a Japanese wig, and her even blacker eyes accusatory, as if no one ever paid or indeed should be drinking at all.

"Ah, there's no money in it," he had once heard her tell his mother. "All these licenses. They were issued when nine million people crowded this island. I'm doing nothing but running a service for a herd of bachelors. The married ones take their wives to Casey's or the Twomeys'." He stood at the bar without speaking and looked at the others, only half-recognizable in the half-light. None spoke. But all nine, one by one, catching his eye, nodded in turn.

"I said what will it be, Paddy?" He looked up at Mrs. Fleming, muttered a semi-apology and asked for a glass of stout, taking a half-pound piece from his snap purse. At the far end of the bar facing him was Tomas Murphy. Was he ninety as well? Some said he had married an English girl in London but left her to return to Sneem alone when she wouldn't accompany him. But Tomas had never confirmed the rumor, which was now fifty years old and worn thin from its frequent recounting. It had become a threadbare statement about a threadbare man. In any event, neither he nor Dennis nor any of the others had a wife in Ireland: the Kelly twins, farriers and mechanics, who lived together over their garage; Shanahan, the barber, who lived in the back of his shop; three day laborers now working the highways, who stood with their backs to the wall exchanging occasional words more like grunts. Burke and Morgan, their backs to the bar, were looking across the room at two hurleys, mounted on the wall, crossed like swords.

"Tim Healy's, I take it," said one. The other took out a gray handkerchief that had once been white, and blew his nose. He returned it to his rear trouser's pocket and picked up his glass. "I know that for a fact," he said.

Paddy heard no more of their conversation. He had hoped that someone his own age might come in. He should have gone to Casey's. He had seen her there once. He held his glass in the air and looked at the men from behind it. They stared into their glasses, turned them meditatively on the soiled counter and occasionally raised them to their lips. All seemed to be half hoping, as Paddy was, that someone would come in, someone of interest. And if that someone did, Paddy knew that they would remain all as they were, and if the newcomer looked at them, as Paddy had, each of them would nod to him.

At this moment, one of the men spoke to Paddy. "Did you say, Paddy Madigan, that the rain had stopped?" He put down the glass he had been raising to his mouth.

"I did not," he said, "but it has."

"I'll move along then," said the questioner. He raised his glass, emptied it, nodded to Mrs. Fleming without speaking, and went out the door. The others hadn't moved. Mrs. Fleming, standing before the cash register, her arms folded across her breasts, waited until the door closed behind the departing customer. Then she stepped to the side and took the man's glass and began to wash it. Impulsively, Paddy picked up his change from the bar and, leaving his glass half-filled, fled the pub.

The rain had begun again. He started the long walk home, past Casey's, past the bakery, past the Protestant church, coming at length to the Catholic presbytery where he saw Father Curtin emerge from the front door and start down the pebbled walk, formally dressed, bearing a large black umbrella. Again on impulse, Paddy ran forward and faced him as he passed through the small black iron gate.

"Good afternoon, Father," he said, touching his cap, determined to speak to a man whose reserve had always intimidated him.

"Paddy! Well, how are you? And your mother, how is she? I hope the rain has not made her arthritis any the worse. We've had quite a siege of it."

"Yes, Father. No, Father," Paddy said. "I mean she's as well as ever."

"Thank God for that. Ah then, I bid you good afternoon."

"Please, Father, it's me. I'm not well."

"Not well! Here, get under my umbrella. Don't be standing there in the rain. Not well? What is the trouble?"

"Father . . ." Paddy began, paused, swallowed and began again. "Father," he said, "I want to get married."

Paddy saw the tall, angular priest look down at him and he sensed distress in the eyes behind the spectacles.

"Oh, dear," Father Curtin said. "Oh, dear!" looking down at his pocket watch and returning it to his vest.

"Come inside, Paddy," he said. "We can dry you off a bit and hear all about it."

Paddy followed the priest as he turned and led the way back into the presbytery. Once before Paddy had been there and it had frightened him: the carpets, and all the books, the leather chairs and the newspapers, some of them in a foreign language. He stood with the priest in the hallway. The opening and closing of the door a second time had brought Mary, the housekeeper, around the corner from the kitchen, but a wave of Father's Curtin's hand sent her back.

"And do you have a young lady?" the priest asked, placing his umbrella in the brass stand. "There are very few in town."

"No," Paddy answered. "That's it. I asked Bessie Thompson to go walking with me and she couldn't. She has to study."

Father Curtin retrieved the umbrella from the stand. "Aye! She's at the training college and will probably go to Dublin for graduate studies. I don't like to say it, but I fear we will lose her to brighter climes."

He looked at Paddy, a head shorter and twice as husky, and Paddy saw in the angular face an anguish to match his own. He focused his questioning eyes on those of the priest until the priest raised his hand to adjust his spectacles and turned his head aside. "Paddy," he said. "Oh, Paddy! You have your little farm and you have your mother, and you'll have to take care of her. It's a poor living, Paddy, although it seems it should do better than it does. It would be hard to bring another woman into that little house, Paddy, if I know your mother. The girls today—there are so many opportunities for them in Dublin or London as teachers, nurses, social workers and secretaries—God knows they're better off in Ireland than in England. Sure, they have no stomach for the hard work of the farm." He paused and looked at his watch again.

"God forbid that you should lose your mother, but if you did and you worked that farm—well, if you could raise a few more cows, or had a part-time government job like Johnny Duggan . . . You understand me, do you? Paddy, you're still a young man—far from thirty, am I right? The future can hold a good deal. Here, I mustn't keep you. I'm off to the council meeting. Are you walking back home? In the rain! Take my umbrella. There, bring it back to me Sunday when you come in for mass. There, there, do not argue. I have Mary's for myself." And they left together.

Paddy stood and watched the tall black figure move down the street with the small red umbrella above him, swaying incongruously, like an exotic, alien flower. Something impelled him to return to the Long Bar, something he dreaded, that ate at him. He would be late for dinner, but let that be. He walked slowly under the large black umbrella, hearing the rain splatter on it angrily. At the door of the pub, he closed the umbrella, shook it before entering and stood it inside the snug. He was determined this time to finish his glass of stout since it would come from the bicycle money.

When he entered, the rank at the bar had decreased by one. Seven men were still there, their glasses before them, like translucent chalices, while Mrs. Fleming was caught in the reflected light from a large silver tureen above her head, the rays sifting around her like an aureole on a hideous idol. His eyes were so affected by the light crowning her that again at first he had difficulty in making out the features of the men as they stood in their solemn lonely ritual. Now he could see them, and he was not surprised that they had turned to stone.

2

HE STARTED BACK under a mere hint of rain, resenting the lowering skies, when, as if in response to his hope, they parted, letting the late afternoon sun stream through. It couldn't raise his heart. The ache continued and a worm of terror moved in his mind. The sense of entrapment came back to him and involuntarily he waved his arms like those of a scarecrow, as he had once cast off a netting of cobwebs that had caught him in a corner of the barn. Spiders. They were waiting for him in the center somewhere to suck his life away. A man he did not recognize drove past him on a tractor, its huge rubber tires spurting water behind them like the spurs of a giant yellow cock. The driver, who must have seen him from afar waving his arms, stared down at him but did not speak. Nor did Paddy. He raised his left arm in a salute and walked on, conscious for the first time that his wellingtons were uncomfortable, not designed for a long walk. He reached the top of the hill and the wind and the sun were drying his jacket and trousers.

At the crest he paused to gaze down across the Sullivan

farmland and pasture and Michael Sullivan's new white house standing beside the old stone one-room affair, once a human habitation but now a shelter for cows. Eithne Sullivan came out of the white house with a pail in her hand, walked over to the chicken enclosure and threw handfuls of grain to the scampering fowl. He watched her bare arm in its muscular gesture, saw her empty the pail, and raise a hand to brush back the tumble of blue-black hair at her forehead. She had come from Kenmare five years ago, a city girl in love with country life, and already had two children, both boys, Michael and John. If ever he had a son he would call him John. John was a strong name, a man's name, a name that no one ever said with a half sneer as they said "Paddy."

"There's a typical Paddy," he heard an English tourist say one day in the center of town when half a hundred men and women left the bus to use the public toilets, walk about the town and photograph the stone bridge and the white octagonal tower of the Protestant church. His gaze went from the Sullivan farm back to the road. Beyond his turning, he saw one of the caravans of the traveling people on the slope of the hill. His mother wouldn't like that. She still called them tinkers, which they were asked not to do.

He began the descent to his home. Turning at last into the pier road, he moved past the summer house of the Dublin solicitor, then up a slight incline and over the wooden stile into his own yard. Two of the chickens ran to him but he shooed them off and stopped for the dog, Zeke, that nuzzled its collie's head into his hand. The dark green door of the ancient stone house stood open and he walked in without a word. Whatever he said, he knew, would be used against him, twisted somehow. The kitchen was empty but his mother shortly entered from her bedroom.

"Have ye no mercy, staying out all hours an' leaving me to deal with the cows?"

She was small and wrinkled, her gray hair matted on her head and pulled back in a bun. Her skin was grayish and black in the depth of the wrinkles, and her green eyes, half glazed over, were all but hidden in a squint. Her lips were thrust out in a perpetual pursing so that he could not see the strong brown teeth. She could chew bones with them, and her step, like her mind, was quicker than his. He did not know why he was afraid of her. She had a habit of shaking her head from side to side after she had spoken, as if driving the words across the intervening space between them and sinking them into his heart.

"It was raining," he said.

"Isn't that a wonder now," she said, "raining in Kerry. Perhaps I had better write the bishop." Her voice had a whine in it that seemed to remain in the air after the words had died. Wagging her head from side to side, she caught up a bowl and filled it with stew from a large iron pot on the back of the black stove. While he hung his cap and jacket on pegs near the door, she put the bowl on the table, darted into a small closet and brought out brown bread and butter.

"I thought it might stop. I waited."

"And where did you think I'd be with the cow? In some fancy Dublin theater?"

He sat down to the stew and bread but couldn't bring himself to eat until he had sat for a moment with his head in his hands.

"But they pushed you out of the pub at last, did they?"

He continued to eat.

"Did she have to ask you to leave?"

"She's never asked me to leave."

"What took you in there at that time of day, at all?"

He raised his aching face to her where she stood over him. "I want to get married," he said.

She stared at him aghast and fell back a step.

"Married," she cried. "You can forget about marriage. Ah, what is it anyways? One good night and you can have the rest of it."

He turned back to his stew, picked up a piece of brown bread and then put it down again. Tears came to his eyes and he wiped them away before he resumed eating.

"You ain't serious, Paddy," she said. "You're a child."

"I'm older than Michael Sullivan was when he took Eithne O'Connell." His voice rose in a tone of wrath.

"Well, find yourself a woman with a hundred acres and a thousand cows."

Her whine had a touch of a snarl in it. She sat in a chair beside the stove and took up some knitting. He ate on in silence, too shattered to speak, wanting to go to bed and rise the next day and perhaps find a different world. When he finished he rose, washed the bowl and the spoon and put one in the cupboard and the other in a drawer. She had turned on the radio and continued to knit. Without a word to her, he went out into the twilight and scuffed his way to the vegetable garden. He swung open the movable section of the wire fence and let himself in, standing for a moment to survey the small plot, then stooping to pluck a few weeds. Zeke came to the fence and pressed his nose against it. He returned the dog's stare for a moment, half inclined to smile, but then returned to his work, finally falling on his knees at the far corner, his hands held behind his head.

What a bollocks he had made of it. He would go to town again Sunday and wait for her again and talk to her again. He should have talked to her before asking her to go out; he had been too abrupt. He would wear his leather shoes and not be tramping like a tinker's child. And his best suit.

A surly sound came to him over the cackling of the hens. He rose from his knees and brushed his trousers, shook the soil from them, and walked out of the vegetable patch.

"I'm coming," he said. "I was getting a few weeds up."

"You're going to march them two bullocks up to Mulcahy the Thief, first thing in the morning. Half seven at the latest."

"Is it tomorrow he goes in?"

"Is it stupid you are?"

He sighed, went in and turned up the radio. A lively jig was playing. He jumped to turn it down. Somehow the music seemed obscene. The silence was easier.

Then out of the silence she came at him again. "It was the priest who put you up to this."

He said nothing.

"Wasn't it now? Ya see, ye don't answer."

"He didn't."

"Yer lying."

"God's truth. He didn't, I tell you."

She had dropped her knitting now and was wagging her head, her purple lips pursed and twitching. She rose quickly and faced him.

"Ye went and told him some dirty things in the box and he told ye. . ."

"He did not." His voice rose in rage and then fell back to a near whisper. "He told me to stay here on the farm with you."

She stared at him for a long moment, her little pig eyes glaring in her twitching head. "It's the money. He's after the money."

"What money?"

She paused before replying. "Yer the only one here fool enough to pay him. They're all the same, them priests. Didn't they bleed your father and him dead, demanding mass money?"

"It's nothing. It's a donation."

"What right have they to it? Let them work! Let him get it from his rich friends. Him with his high-falutin' ideas, reading them dirty French newspapers and talking Irish. I curse him. I spit upon the likes of him."

He turned on her in anger and sorrow and with a sense of horror. "Ma! You mustn't talk like that. You mustn't. You'll have an attack."

Her face was now as purple as her lips.

"Christ damn them," she cried, waving her right hand in circles over her head. "Putting those ideas into yer head."

"He didn't," he shouted, grasping her arm and bringing it down. "He only lent me his umbrella."

The incongruity of it checked her tirade.

"Umbrella? What for? Where is it?"

She looked around.

"I left it in the pub. Sure, I'll get it Sunday and fetch it to him."

"And did he give it to ye to cover me while I chased the cows?"

He sat down again with a sense of fatigue. Behind him he could hear that she was back at her knitting. After a long silence, he remarked pacifically, "An itinerant's caravan is sitting on the hill."

"They're the devil's craytures," she said. "They steal more than the priests and there's no work in them either."

"Will you not be going on about the priests!" he said in irritation, and then he realized it was a mistake to revive the subject.

"What good are they anyways, snooping about? Oh, there's a lot I could tell ye about them, with their whoring and their drink."

"Whoring? For God's sake, Ma, I tell you it's a subject you're daft on!"

"If you didn't listen to them you'd not be calling your own mother daft."

"You know what I mean."

"And ye know what I mean. They're no good! One of them trying to get at me."

"God, you know that's not so."

"Well, he would have if I went near him. Oh, I know them, right enough. Marry! You! Oh, they'll marry ye for ten pounds and douse yer children for a quid and say, 'God be with ye,' and 'God damn ye,' under their breath. The cannyballs know what to do with them. They boil them alive."

Despite his heartache and anger, Paddy had to smile to himself.

"I think I'll walk to the shore," he said. "I've been piling up some seaweed and the ass and I will bring it up tomorrow."

"Mind the bullocks," she said. "They come afore the seaweed."

As he went out the door, he could hear her mutter and then cry, "God's curse on the lot of them!"

3

THUNK! THUNK! THUNK!

The second blow of the cudgel knocked her down. The third caught her on the legs as she scuttled under the caravan out of the reach of her father panting above her from exertion and rage. He teetered for a moment and then threw the cudgel after her but the fold of her great plaid blanket turned the blow. She didn't cry; she waited for him to move away, back to the place beside the smoldering fire where he had left the bottle of poteen. But he stood where he was.

"Why in Christ's name am I cursed with the care of ye?" His voice was a rasp and a gurgle as if his throat were half filled with phlegm. His blue eyes were bloodshot under the greasy felt hat beneath which strands of dirty black hair showed randomly. Still teetering, he hitched up his sagging trousers, belted with a piece of rope, shifted his powerful shoulders inside the soiled tweed jacket and turned to walk away. Then he paused, stooped and picked up the coins she had passed to him and he had thrown on the ground.

"Come back tomorrow with half a quid," he said, "and

I'll show ye a true beatin'." He coughed, spat and walked to the fire.

She lay now so she could see across the road, down over the sweep of green pastures, erratically lined into polygons by stone walls, loosely piled, and ranks of stakes with barbed wire, hemming in the black and white cattle. In the distance the river spread like a gigantic silver tray, and across it, on the far bank, the sunlight fell in an isolated patch of gold-green grassland.

She dreamed she was in a boat, sailing away, away. She had never been in a boat or a motor car. She had been in a bus but it had not been moving. Her father sent her to beg into those towns where the enormous tourist buses stopped to let the passengers visit the pubs or photograph the countryside, a view of the misty mountains or the boiling river, or the townsfolk or herself. Often she had been paid to pose, but the folks in Sneem resented her, and several told her to clear out. Tinkers are not welcome in the little towns, nor in the cities for that matter, but they leave you alone in the cities. She remembered Galway fondly.

She had never known any home except the caravan, which had once been very pretty and cozy. It had been decorated with red and green stripes and yellow flowers when she was small and her mother was alive. They had been happy on the road together, the three of them. She had enjoyed begging through Galway with her mother when she was beyond the carrying stage. She could not remember being carried by her mother when begging, but she remembered vividly walking with her, and later entering some of the shops all by herself, holding out her little box and thanking the occasional donor. She had felt warm when her mother praised her, and she remembered with tears her mother's smile.

"She had a grand smile," she would say aloud to herself when she reflected on the memory, and there was music in the memory of her mother's voice as it called to her, "Jane! Jane! Come now, Jane!" When her mother was alive, her father never struck her, nor could she remember him striking her mother, but that once, even when they drank together and quarreled. Mammy, she called her. Mammy could make him work, buying, selling and trading horses, keeping the caravan greased and painted, and the horse groomed properly and the canvas stitched so the rain wouldn't come in.

Half a dozen tinker families had gathered for Mammy's funeral. Her father went out with two other men and dug the grave, and then they walked into Kilorglin and drank all night, and fought. He had been knocked down and when he stood at the graveside for the priest's prayers and to see the box lowered into the ground his right eye was swollen, discolored and closed. But she remembered the tears on his cheeks as numerous as her own, although he didn't sob the way she sobbed until a huge tinker woman took her in her arms and carried her about, big as she was.

She couldn't remember when the beatings started. She could only count to five. He had thrown a stick at her one day when she had tipped over his whisky bottle so that the poteen ran into the ground. The stick had struck her left eye so that it bled and he took her to a doctor's office, the same doctor who had come to the caravan the night her mother died. They healed the eye but the sight was gone and it was clouded.

"I didn't mean it," he told her in the doctor's office. But later he added cruelly, "You'll beg the better for it."

Another beating had broken her nose, but they saw no

doctor and it set crooked. She had cried herself to sleep that time, and thought of running away. He had been drunk, of course, and he was drunk more often than not these days. Half the time the drunken blows could scarcely be felt, so well did her plaid blanket protect her. It had been her mother's and had concealed her when she was a child in arms. She wore it constantly now and, when she went begging, she dressed her doll and carried it under the blanket as if she bore a real infant. People didn't know the difference for all they could see. Many of the tinker women borrowed a baby when they went out, but she knew no one who would favor her that way. She was conscious that her father was not liked by the other tinkers. It was why they camped alone.

She crawled from under the caravan and went to the fire to stir the soup. He was almost asleep.

"They don't want me in this town," she said.

"To hell with them," he muttered.

She fetched a bowl and ladle from the caravan and scooped some soup into it for her supper. He had made the soup and had taught her to make soup and stew and to cook eggs and bake bread.

Time and again, she yearned to join the other tinkers, especially when she passed a gathering on the road and saw the children scampering about and the women chatting together, so friendly. Chinwagging, they called it. There was a time she and her father talked at length and he told her stories about the tinker life, about her mother and about his great feats of strength, but all that seemed to dry up into chance remarks and drunken growls, or the terrible things he said to her when he came at her in her bed in the caravan at night which she tried not to think about. He had fallen asleep by the fire now, half couched against the black leather harness he had been repairing. She sat watching the sun go down and, with the thickening of the dusk, went into the caravan and lighted a candle. In the flickering yellow aura of light, she began to change the dress on her doll.

4

SUNDAY WAS FAIR and shining. Paddy rose early, fed the hens, mended a bit of fence and went back into the house for his breakfast. His mother put eggs, rashers and bread before him on the tan wood of the table and then poured him tea. He ate with a sense of elation, hurriedly, and then went into his room and donned his good suit, his brown shoes and a white shirt and brown necktie, one of two he owned. He didn't always wear a necktie to mass, nor his good suit either for that matter, but he knew he would see Bessie Thompson and was determined to speak to her.

"Ye might be doin' a bit of fishin' and not runnin' off to church of a mornin' like this. Hypocrites! All of them. Hypocrites!"

He thought of his father. Oh, how he missed his father! His earliest memory was of the two of them, standing in the yard in the evening, the hay piled beside them, and he clinging to his father's trousers. He reached only about the knee, and the worn worsted seemed coarse to his hand. His father's leg seemed as hard and as massive as the oak tree, and his head rose to the stars. Even in his maturity, when he thought of his father, in his mind's eye that man was crowned with stars. Had they walked to the house together that night or had his father carried him as he had so many times? He wasn't sure. He had loved to sit high on his father's shoulders, pretending he was a knight mounted on a mighty horse. He missed the old man's laugh and his strength of personality that dealt so kindly and yet so firmly with the obsessions of his wife. He bore her parsimony with an amused tolerance that was never overbearing to her. Evenings in the kitchen, Paddy remembered how her strange ranting would rock the room, while the old man sat reading the *Kerry Examiner*, seemingly oblivious to the rasping voice Only when she turned to her favorite theme—the greed of the clergy—did he finally take notice.

"Wife!" he would say. "Wife, that'll do."

Her face would grow purple, partly through rage and partly through resentment at being told. And yet he never had to say it twice. Something in the force of his character meant that a threat never had to be taken beyond the verbal stage; a warning did not have to explain itself, or give details. She simply recognized the force of the man's personality, an idiosyncrasy that put the situation on a different plane than it had been on before, that somehow diminished her complaint, and diminished her as well. Long after his father was gone Paddy remembered, but the memory did not help him with his responses to her.

"I'll fish tomorrow," he said.

She moved about the kitchen nervously, making work. She lifted the skillet from the stove and started for the door, only to turn back and replace it on the black surface of the stove, toward the rear away from the heat. That done, she walked back and forth watching him as he straightened his tie and reached for his cap.

"Yer a fool like your father," she fumed.

He made no answer. She settled some loose gray hairs on her bun, readjusting some hairpins, holding one for a moment between her teeth and her pursed lips. When at length she removed it, she said, "Well, don't be givin' any money in the collection. Ye can afford naught."

He took his dish and tea cup from the table where he had left them and put them in the sink.

"It's a grand day," he said, and shifting the cap to the back of his head, he stepped out into the light of the early sun, nervous and hopeful. He had scarce turned into the main road when an automobile stopped and swung open its door. He stepped in beside Mrs. Mulcahy.

"Good morning, Paddy," she said. "It's into mass, is it?"

"It is," he said, "and I'm grateful to your husband for selling the bullocks."

"Sure, it's his business, Paddy. He does it for you, you know. He wouldn't speak to your mother."

Paddy did not answer. They rode on in silence and were soon in the square. The lift from Mrs. Mulcahy made him earlier than he would ordinarily have been. His first thought was to get Father Curtin's umbrella from the Long Bar, but he remembered it would not be opened until after the mass. Immobilized, he stood across the street from the pub struggling in his mind whether to try to get the umbrella and deliver it to the sacristy or to retrieve it after mass and bring it to the presbytery. The important thing was not to let the fetching and delivering of the umbrella interfere with his talking to Bessie Thompson. Better to wait until after mass.

What if Father Curtin spied him in his pew and asked, "Where is my umbrella?" It worried him and he could feel his palms sweat. He swallowed and resolved to go into the church late, just before Father Curtin entered the altar. He would watch from the vestibule to see where Bessie sat so he could sit nearby. His decision made, he left his place on the pavement and walked down the street, a culdesac, at the bottom of which the great gray stone church raised its façade and its single thrilling spire.

He moved slowly, for a group of early arrivals crowded the steps. Half a dozen men were standing in a group at the top of the steps near the side door, the only one used in winter weather; now in spring habit still gave it eminence. He mounted the steps and took his stand in a serrated line of men, nodding wordlessly to those nearest to him. Here he had a vantage view and would see her coming.

Down in the street automobiles were parking diagonally with their noses to the curbing, and when those spaces were taken others parked double. Later arrivals would park in the square and walk in. On both pavements and in the center of the street itself, parishioners were walking toward the church, singly, in twos, and here and there in family groups, the women in bright colors, the men generally in drab shades. At last Paddy saw her. She wore a dark blue cloth coat, three-quarter length, open to show a light blue dress underneath. Over her high forehead was a small round blue hat. She wore white gloves.

As he watched his palms began to sweat again, but the nature of his uneasiness soon altered. She had turned her head to look back over her shoulder toward a tall young man in a smartly tailored gray suit and a felt hat who was just locking the door of a Renault sedan at the edge of the square and was walking hurriedly toward her. When he came beside her, he took her arm in his, and Paddy's heart sank. He knew she had no brother, and the young man's smile, his air of confidence, of protectiveness and his intense attention were telltale. Paddy watched them approach and mount the stairs together, their heads close in conversation. He dropped his head for a second and found himself looking at their black shoes—how shined they were! He raised his head quickly as they neared and, carefully timing his gesture so as to catch her eye, tipped his cap.

"Hello, Bessie!"

"Why, Paddy, good morning."

She smiled and they passed by. The young man with her looked back at him, but Paddy saw no disdain in his glance. He was too excited, too exalted at being called by name, to fret. She had called him by name! He turned and followed them into the church. They proceeded down the middle aisle. The pews to the left were filling up with men and those on the right with women, with a sprinkling of married couples. Bessie genuflected and entered a pew to the right and her escort followed her. Paddy's exaltation sagged as he bent his knee and entered a pew on the left a few feet behind theirs. It's meaningless, he told himself; it needn't mean they have an understanding. But inside him a persistent voice whispered that it meant a lot. The young man was too well dressed. They must have met at some college function. He could feel it in his stomach now, and knew enough to recognize that he was tormenting himself, but he couldn't let go.

The mass slipped by without his noticing it. He did not hear a word of the homily. While Father Curtin preached, Paddy's eyes and thoughts were fixed on her round blue hat and her shoulders and the black hair that curled above them. He became so engrossed in her physical movements, in the devout tilt of her neck, and her walk to the communion rail and her return, that he forgot to go himself until only one or two persons were left at the rail and he was then too embarrassed to hurry up the aisle. He remained in his pew, still staring at her. When the mass ended, he waited until they passed and went out directly behind them.

They paused to talk with friends at the top of the stairs and he tried to stand where again she might notice him, but at last, in nervous disappointment, fearing that he might be observed and laughed at by others, he went down the smooth steps and stood at the bottom. The street was alive with movement and noise, automobiles starting up, groups of men and women chatting, children prancing or playing. Three young boys in knickers and Sunday shoes were playing an erratic game of tag, running between the standing groups or circling them. At length Bessie and her escort came down the steps, both smiling, but they passed Paddy without seeing him, although he had stepped forward to be in their line of vision. He set out after them, walked rapidly past them, and then looked back and tipped his cap. She looked up and saw him but seemed to make no sign of recognition except for the shadow of a nod. The three romping boys ran between Paddy and the couple, panting and shouting, and headed up the street.

At the top of the street, on the corner of the main street, Paddy could see a tinker girl sitting against the side of the building, her small cardboard box on the pavement before her. Several of the churchgoers had dropped the odd penny or two as they passed. Others looked at her resentfully and behind him he heard a man say loudly, "It's a disgrace letting them beg. Why can't the Gardai get her out of there?"

At this moment one of the romping boys, running along the pavement, quite deliberately kicked the box, upsetting it and scattering the money. Paddy was only a few feet away from her when it happened. He sensed he should do something but stood rooted in indecision. Suddenly, he saw Bessie's escort spring past him, his shiny shoes flashing in the late morning sun, and saw him overtake the guilty boy and, grabbing him by the ear, march him back to the pavement where the box had spilled. The tinker girl, hugging a concealed infant form beneath her blanket with one arm, was recovering the scattered coins with the other. The tall young man stood by while the boy picked up the rest of the coins and the box and restored them to their former place. Near as he was Paddy could not hear what any of the parties to the incident said, but Bessie's voice came from behind him.

"Oh, Reggie," she said, "that was well done. That was a mean thing for that boy to do. He deserved having his ear tweaked."

"I've no love for the traveling people, Bess," Reggie said, "but I can't stand that sort of cruelty. Young blackguard!"

Still rooted to the pavement, Paddy watched the two of them go on to their sedan. Without glancing at him, they entered the car and, with Reggie at the wheel, drove off. Paddy, having watched them go, turned and looked at the tinker girl, who was once again propped against the wall, the box in front of her but closer than it had been before. He was trying to sort out in his head the thrust of all that had happened. The girl looked up at him, surprising him at first with the arctic stare of her bad eye. He concealed his shock at the sight of it, but was slow to take his glance from her weather-worn face, the large blue eye, the twisted nose and the thick red hair.

Conscious of his scrutiny, she smiled and the white even teeth and the crinkling of her face somehow transformed her appearance. Involuntarily, Paddy smiled back and then in embarrassment tipped his cap and walked away, knowing her blue eye was fixed on him. He stopped and searched his pockets for coins, coming up with two one-pence pieces. He paused for a moment but couldn't find the courage to go back and throw them in the box. He would buy a newspaper for his mother, have a drink at the Long Bar, reclaim the priest's umbrella, deliver it to the presbytery and go home.

But, oh, why couldn't he have chased the scamp who kicked the box and brought him back by the ear to make amends and have heard that lilting voice say, "Oh, Paddy, that was well done! Well done, Paddy."

The pub had opened and all the customers had yet to be served. Mrs. Fleming was behind the bar, and her son Eamon, who was helping, soon came to Paddy.

"I'll take a pint," said Paddy, "but I've come for my umbrella."

"Umbrella?"

"I left it here a few nights back." He had the time wrong.

"Hey, Mum! Have ye got Paddy Madigan's umbrella?"

"Is it you that left it? You're a long time coming after it, and aren't you the fancy one now, carrying an umbrella."

The conversation brought a dozen sets of eyes to where Paddy was standing at the bar. He felt his face flush.

"I have the loan of it," he said. He wanted to make a joke of it, but could go no further. Something about it being Lent, although it wasn't. Mrs. Fleming had wandered off and now returned with the umbrella and passed it to him over the counter.

"Maybe you'll be seeing Bessie Thompson home with it," said Eamon, grinning at him.

The stout soured in his mouth and he gulped in

embarrassment. Were there no secrets in the bloody village? But although he knew that the proper answer to Eamon's question might save him from cruel abasement, he could not think of a clever reply. With a shaky bravado that barely hid the tumult inside him, he said, "Ah, she's spoken for." Eamon laughed aloud and tossed his curly head in what Paddy felt was gesture of ridicule. He took the umbrella and his glass to a table near the jukebox and ignored the conviviality at the bar.

5

THE BUS ARRIVED at high noon, glossy and green, its chrome sparkling in the sunlight, and turned with a dust-swirling swoop into the parking area beside the shops. Jane stood with her doll clutched under the dark plaid blanket, holding the cardboard cookie box in her right hand. Her thick red hair was still matted after the early shower but her high brown leather boots had dried. The windows of the bus were open and even as it drew up she could hear the metallic voice of the driver over the amplifier addressing the tourists.

"You have an hour here, my friends. There are two restaurants and half a dozen pubs all happy to serve you. The public toilets are directly behind us here. I will lock up the bus so you can leave your valuables. You'll see one of the itinerants begging. Give her nothing. They're a nuisance to the country. Happy eating."

The first passengers began getting off before his last words were spoken. Jane moved near to them holding out the box. A woman with her hair in curlers under a kerchief and wearing a white hand-knit jumper and gray slacks drew quickly away as she left the bus. A young girl in a blue jumper and pleated skirt, a camera in hand, said to Jane, "Do you mind if I photograph you?"

Without answering, Jane thrust the box at her. The girl looked over her shoulder in the direction of the driver, who had not yet left his seat, and then reaching into her leather satchel, brought out ten pence and dropped it in the box. Jane stood in silence and then smiled for the camera. The bus was emptying rapidly and two other tourists raised their cameras and photographed her. She thrust out the box at them. They seemed intent on ignoring it. "Please give!"

A tall man with a hooked nose and close-set eyes reached into his pocket, but the woman with him laid a hand on his arm. "The driver said it's a no-no."

"Oh yeah?"

"Didn't you hear him?"

"It's all right," said Jane. "Please give. For the baby."

"Ah, what the hell," said the man. He dropped in two pence and turned away. The others passed her by. Patiently she followed one group of women around the square, approaching them as they looked in a shop window. One diminutive, aged woman with white hair, a stooped back and a cane turned to her and said, "Please go away." Slowly Jane turned and walked across the square toward the public toilets. Selecting a dry place against the wall, she sat down in the sun with her box before her on the ground. She readjusted the doll beneath her blanket so that the human hair (her mother's) barely showed. She put the ten pence in her pocket and left the coppers on the white bottom of the shallow box. She leaned against the wall and closed her eyes.

The sun was blessedly warm. She felt snug and comfortable and could almost sleep. For more than half an hour she sat with her eyes closed, hearing footsteps come and go, opening her eyes only when a coin fell in the box. "God bless you." A ten-pence from a woman, two-pence pieces from another woman. The same from a man, and a farthing from a child. She was far from her goal. Earlier she had gone into the shops but the word had been passed around by the merchants to give her nothing. One woman shopkeeper had taken up a rolled newspaper and with blows driven her out. Then she had gone to the pubs. The publicans usually ordered her out as soon as they saw her. At Casey's she went in quietly. Five men were at the bar, three in conversation, and the other two by themselves. She put out the box to the talkers. They ignored her and she moved toward the other two.

"Casey," one called, "give the lady a glass of stout."

"For God's sake, Tim, we don' t want the likes of her in here. Whatever are you doing!"

"Ah, sure, I'd give her no money but I'll always stand a lady a drink."

"By God, you've got a strange definition of a lady."

The glass of stout was put before her, and, smiling her thanks and muttering, "May God bless you," she took it and walked to a table in a dark corner and sat. It was a pleasant moment in the day.

At another pub she had no sooner entered than the young, fat, red-faced barkeeper shouted, "Out! Out! Out!" and kept shouting until she left. She walked to the bridge and watched the frothy torrent tumbling over the knot of rocks in the middle of the stream and at length turned to meet the next incoming bus.

When the second bus had gone, she found she had accumulated two shillings less than a pound. She had stood by the passengers as they alighted and then walked and sat against the wall, her eyes closed. She dreamed of a white cottage by the seashore. What would it be like to live in one? She had twice been in such houses, but never beyond the front room. Some of the itinerants had gone to live in houses built by the government but when she met others on the roads they told her that the ones who had done so were not happy. The children were ill treated in the schools, particularly if they chose not to go regularly.

When her mother had suggested schooling for her, her father had always responded roughly, "Those schools can fix a girl bad. They're no place for a girl, or a good lad either." She couldn't read, although her father could. He had started to teach her but after her mother's death, when his drinking got worse, he had stopped and refused her any training. He had started to teach her to count, but then had stopped that too, except to have her recognize coins and bills. There was a pound and there was a half pound and there were ten pence pieces, and if she counted five twice she had a pound. For a long while she had thought that ten was less than five. When she had worked out the value of coins, she stopped bothering.

He had taught her to fish, to trap birds, to knit and to sew, and one heavenly day to row a punt. She could tend the horse and had milked the cow when they had one. Other tinker women had taught her various things about cooking and cleaning herself and dressing. She had loved the tinker meetings when several families would get together. But all that had stopped about the same time he had started to come at her in her bed. The thought of it made her shiver. She sensed that the other tinkers knew and because of it would have nothing to do with him. He was an outcast among the tinkers, and maybe an outlaw. He frightened her. The beatings were preferable. Some day she would run away.

Two buses came in, one behind the other. She rose quickly and went over to stand beside them. If she collected over a pound she would go to one of the shops, without telling him, and buy some milk and a cake. She would have liked to enter one of the restaurants and sit down at one of the nice clean tables, the ones with the napery and the silver and eat a meal and some tea and scones or a trifle. But neither restaurant would admit her. The buses had scarcely begun to empty when a sudden shower came. The tourists scampered for cover, to the toilets, to the pubs, to the restaurants. To her delight a running man threw her a half pound. Now she had enough, but a sense of obligation kept her waiting for the passengers to return to the bus, or for the rain to stop. She crouched in the doorway of a private house. At the end of the hour, the rain still fell and the passengers hurried into the buses. She would go for her milk and cake. Some day if a lot of silver fell and they were in a big town, she would go to the cinema. She had never been.

6

ONE DAY NO MONEY at all; the town was sick of her and she of it and of the rain. Behind her the empty church was dark. Little light came through the stained glass windows because the clouds had banished the sun entirely, and the wind from the west seemed to carry more and more bleakness across the sky. Her eyes were becoming accustomed to the dark, for it was fifteen minutes since she had taken refuge in the church from the downpour. The lock on the wooden box was a trivial thing. She slipped the sliver of rusted nail through the loop, paused for a second to look behind her, and seeing no one, twisted the nail and broke the lock. She removed it and was now able to raise the wooden lid of the box with its donations for the poor and thrust her right hand inside. The cool of the coins welcomed her fingers. There must have been a dozen of them, and by the feel at least one half pound was among them. She started to draw them out and then she screamed.

A strong male hand had grasped her wrist, holding it tightly against the sharp edge of the box. Where had he come from? She had heard nothing. Although she had been surprised and had screamed she was not frightened. This had happened before and usually ended with a cuff on the ear or a kick in the arse. She turned her head and looked up into the thin face of Father Curtin, his eyes hidden by some dim light and shadow on the spectacles, giving him a sinister appearance.

"You shouldn't be stealing, my pretty girl," he said, still holding her hand against the edge of the box so that her wrist hurt, and she dropped the coins she had taken. At the sound of their fall, he released her hand and resettled the cover on the box, stooped and picked up the broken lock and stood, towering over her, tall and angular, tossing the broken lock up and down menacingly in his hand. She looked stolidly at him, still hearing the word "pretty" sound in her head again and again like an echo. No one had ever called her "pretty" and the ambiguity of the usage escaped her.

"Do you not get enough with your begging and the dole that you have to steal?" His voice sounded bitter.

"My da beats me," she said, "if I don't bring him enough money for the drink."

"And what is your name?"

"Jane," she said, "Jane Ward."

"Jane. I see. How long have you been on the roads?"

"All my life."

"How old are you?"

She shrugged.

"Have you been to school at all?"

She shook her head. "My da says the schools are fixing girls bad."

The priest stared at her for a full minute in silence.

"Now," he said, "I want you to tell me the truth. Do you understand? It's a dreadful thing to lie to a priest."

She nodded and raised her right hand to wipe her nose on the back of it. The doll was still clutched under her shawl.

"Do you understand?"

"I do."

"Have you stolen anything else in Sneem?"

She shook her head.

"Are you sure?"

She nodded.

"Tell me."

"I've stolen naught."

He closed his hand tightly on the broken lock. "How many days have you been in town?"

"Four days this day."

"Has your father beaten you every day?"

She nodded again and, seeing the anguish on his face, spoke in a rush. "Ah, sure, it's not like it's bad, father. He always hits me through the blanket. He's not hit me on the head since he damaged my eye."

She raised her head with the blind eye to him so in the half-light he could see it and the dirt smeared on her face and the twisted nose.

"Ye'll not send me to the Gardai!"

He reached into the box and took out the coins and put all the pieces into her hand without counting them, and then reaching into his pocket, he took out a pound note and passed it to her. In managing the coins and the note she dropped the doll. He stooped, picked it up and passed it back to her.

"He'll not beat you tonight."

She looked at him in wonder.

"But promise me you'll steal no more." And then: "Have you stolen from churches before?"

"I have not," she said, "My da doesn't like churches.

He says they're bad luck. He will not let me go."

"Are you all he has?"

She nodded and smiled up at him. "There's just me. Mammy died long ago."

Father Curtin had his back to her and was examining the broken clasp. She had put the money in her pocket and was rearranging the doll under the blanket.

"I say my prayers," she said.

"God welcomes that."

"Can I go now?"

"You may," he said.

"Thank you for your kindness."

"Try not to steal," he said.

She watched him turn toward a side aisle, taking the lock out again and tossing it in his hand. Turning herself, she pushed open the large leather-covered, brass-studded swinging door and went out. Before the door stopped swinging, she went running back. She was racked with agony, and could feel hot tears on her cheeks.

"Father," she cried, "I want to run away!"

"Run away! Where?" He turned back toward her.

"Ah," she whispered, "anywhere."

He raised his left hand to his forehead and with his right thrust the lock back into a pocket of his trousers. She looked up at him, one eye burning in pain, the other dead in its socket. The doll fell to the floor.

"He fucks me!"

With a succession of sobs, she threw herself into his arms. "My father!" she cried. "He fucks me!"

She felt the arms of the priest around her, and she clung wildly to him, her sobs mounting in intensity, alternating at last with shrieks that might have come from an animal in excruciating pain, caught in a trap.

7

THE RAIN, MILD and warm, came and went. Clouds, like clusters of fugitives in inky capes, raced across the sky propelled by the first hot wind of spring. It was a day to be walking, a day to leave the farm and get into town and see one's friends and neighbors, to move in and out of the pubs furthering the gossip and the news, or merely to stand elbow to elbow, amiable and taciturn in the quiet exchange of companionship. That sort of thing could ease the ache in Paddy's heart, an ache that ran through his body. For he had been told that the banns of marriage would soon be announced for Bessie Thompson and Reginald Blake, who, some said, was English, some said was American, and all said, was rich. Why would a girl not yet out of training college be after marrying a man unless he was one of the gentry with money no object? He would find a pub where they weren't talking about her.

His heart had been somewhat eased by a request that he join the local hurling team. Not that the honor was that great or that his skill, despite his strength, was that extraordinary. The team always had difficulty getting a full complement for its matches against the teams of the other Kerry towns. But—Paddy was conscious of it if no one else was—there was not another man on the team who had not finished his schooling. The ages ran from sixteen to thirty-six. The diurnal duties that were necessary if some of the older men were to eat and keep their families in food necessitated a "bench" of players who could be called on when the regulars were elsewhere. But Paddy, at twenty, husky and strong, had never been called upon for the bench. He was awkward and slow. But now the invitation had come and it pleased him. His mother had merely laughed when he told her, a half-laugh, half-whine, that told him precisely what she thought of it all and that she would resent whatever time it took away from the farm. "It's nonsense, nonsense," she said. "Grown men beating themselves with sticks and the priests encouraging it."

She was sitting in the kitchen knitting, with her pursed lips twitching, and her head wagged the last words at him. Wednesday would be practice day and he would have to arrange his chores to suit the time. Donnelly offered to pick him up, and so he left his hurly and his shoes and his shirt in Donnelly's car. Today there was no practice. Today was just a blaze of burgeoning, blossoming spring and a warm sun for the town. He would drink today at Casey's for he was sure Mrs. Fleming at the Long Bar talked to his mother. How, he did not know, with no telephone in the house; and as a rule he saw the mail. God knows there was little of it. Of course, his mother walked to town occasionally. But he remembered Eamon's slur in the Long Bar when he went for the umbrella. So he had Casey's in mind when he neared the square. He had on his great sweater despite the sun and his working boots and two pounds in his pocket. If Bessie was to be married, the bicycle could wait. When her image loomed in his mind, he ached; then he shrugged and tried to think of tomorrow's chores.

He swung down a slight incline into the square and stopped in some surprise to see groups of men and women standing on the pavement watching a disorder in the street. Near him was a salesman who had just delivered bread to Campbell's grocery and was shutting the rear doors of his van.

"What's here?" Paddy asked.

"Ah," said the man, turning to Paddy. "The boys found that the tinker's infant is no baby at all but a stuffed doll. They're using it as a football."

The scene fell into focus for Paddy. Four young men—two of them older than he—were tossing the doll with its red hair from one to another. Jane stood in the center of their grouping, darting first at one man only to have him toss the doll to another at the last moment. When she ran to that man he would throw the doll to a third. Now she paused and one of the men held the doll out tantalizingly toward her. She walked slowly toward him until she was about two feet away and then lunged to get the doll. He snatched it back and threw it over her head to another. She, in turn, responded quickly to his movement and by twisting suddenly tried to catch the doll as it went above her, but slipped and fell. She rose slowly and readjusted her cumbersome blanket, too much for a hot day. When she fell, her red hair had loosened from the bun in which it had been caught up and was now hanging about her shoulders. Paddy caught sight of her sweating face and the suffering written on it. The crowd was mixed in its attitude, some laughing at the horseplay and some shaking their heads in disapproval.

"Give it to her," someone cried.

"Quick," another shouted, "she's coming!"

"It's not right to torment the poor soul," a woman said. "But why is she here? She should be in Galway or Kilorglin or beyond."

Paddy watched for a moment, his eyes scrunched, his face flushed. There was something wrong about it all. His sympathy for the girl—she was a grown woman—bubbled inside him and he started to turn away. But there was a fascination in the conflict that brought him back. He remembered Sunday when the running boy had kicked her box and Reggie—or whatever his name was—had darted forward and caught the guilty boy by the ear. Paddy looked at the four lads tossing the doll about. Two of the tormentors were members of the hurling team. He had practiced with them several times: Tomas Cronin, exuberant, a strong man, twenty-five years old, and Joseph Branca, a lithe, spirited athlete, about the same age, always ready for a jape or a prank or a punch. Paddy was reluctant to challenge them, either or both; they seemed much more mature. But the ache in the bottom of his head pointed like a direction finder. He ran forward and stood in the circle, gesturing for the doll to be thrown to him. The girl was tired now, and moved slowly toward Cronin, who was swinging the doll by its hair. She straightened the blanket on her shoulders and sprang toward him. Cronin tossed it in the air to Paddy. Paddy caught the doll with shaking hands and, feeling overwhelmingly self-conscious before the crowd, walked to within two feet of the girl and threw the doll into her arms.

"What the hell are you up to, Paddy?" Branca yelled, passing his hand through his tangled hair and walking quickly and threateningly toward Paddy. Still trembling, Paddy looked him directly in the eye. "You've had your fun," he said. "Leave her be."

"What's she to you?"

"Naught."

"That was a damned funny trick, Paddy." It was Cronin who had come up. The crowd was drifting away, but some stayed in anticipation of more excitement.

"I don't know her," said Paddy. "It just didn't seem right, she being a woman and all."

"She shouldn't be begging in this town," said Cronin, "and pretending the doll was a baby."

Paddy was slow to answer, but his eyes were still on them, one then another. At last he said slowly, "I know."

The three men stood without speaking for a minute. The two younger tormentors had moved up beside them. All the interchange was now in the eyes.

"Aye," said Cronin, the oldest, at length, "I see what you mean. I'll buy you a jar."

The younger pair ran off. Branca, Cronin and Paddy turned into Casey's bar. Behind them the tinker girl, the doll clutched to her breast with both hands, walked north toward the main road and the far-off slope where stood her caravan. No one had said, "That was well done, Paddy," and Bessie Thompson would never know or care and what was a tinker's thank-you but a hollow thing even if it came? In the pub the incident was soon forgotten. Hurling talk was the order of the day. Casey was at his conversational best. Cronin and Branca now believed that Paddy had done them a favor and the prospects of the team soared with each additional drink.

"By God," said Paddy, "I must get home. I have a week's fill of chores."

"Don't forget Wednesday, Paddy. Half-one at the field."

"I'm your man," said Paddy, and he left. Raising his

hand to a passing automobile, he was quick to get a lift from an American tourist going north after doing the Ring of Kerry. Two miles out Paddy left the car. He had seen the tinker girl sitting by the side of the road. He walked slowly back to where she was sitting, and saw her watching his approach.

"I'm sorry about what happened."

She looked up at him and smiled. "It's all right," she said. "I'm all right now."

"I saw you sitting here and I thought you might have been hurt."

"No, it's just . . . when I get home."

"What's when you get home?"

"My da," she said.

Paddy had a faint memory of town gossip. "He beats you?"

"Beats me?" A long pause. "He does. He beats me."

Paddy looked down at his shoes and shuffled them in the gravel. "Why do you let him? Is he big?"

"He's my Da."

"And he beats you."

She nodded.

"Come," he said, "I'll go with you and tell him he can't."

Without rising, she shook her head, and her lungs heaved a great breath. "He'd pay you no mind."

"Come and let's see."

"I can't speak ill of my Da."

"You've spoken no ill of him. Come on."

She rose, the doll clutched beneath her blanket, and they walked along together.

"Isn't that blanket too hot?"

She took it off and wrapped the doll in it. "I get used to it."

Paddy was conscious of two things. She had beautiful red hair, and the blanket smelled like a chicken yard. He was very aware of smells. Rashers cooking. His mother's teeth and breath. Pleasant and unpleasant. The smell from the woman beside him seemed to come out of the very soil, out of the beginning of the world, a stink. It put him off even in his talk. He thought to himself, she must never wash, or maybe it's all in the blanket. His nose became inured to the odor and to his astonishment he lost all sense of it in their conversation.

She had a slight speech impediment that twisted the "r's" on her tongue, but it went unnoticed when she talked of the countryside and how she loved it. She had her own names for all the flowers and they talked of fishing and laughed about the great grey heron that haunted the cove and fled on wide lumbering wings when they came in sight of him. When they reached the crest of the hill and started down toward the slope where the caravan stood, she stopped.

"You'd better not come," she said.

"I'm not afraid," he said.

"You ain't?"

They went down the hill and up the slope side by side. A fire was smoldering under a large copper kettle. The dog was curled under the caravan, too old and too tired to move. The rear doors of the caravan stood open.

"Da!" And again, louder, "Da!"

She walked up the rear steps of the caravan and looked in, standing for a moment in silence. He saw her reach and put the doll inside. She then turned to Paddy, who stood quietly a few feet away. He saw an appeal in her posture and moved forward. Looking inside, he saw a man prostrate on the floor, an empty bottle beside him.

"He's drunk," she said. "Dead drunk."

"That's terrible," said Paddy.

"No," she smiled, "that's better."

He felt disappointed. He had seen himself again as a hero in her eyes, confronting her Da, warning him that he was not to strike his daughter. All was now anti-climax. He was reduced to awkwardness, unable to speak. The old dog raised himself at last and came over and licked Jane's hand. With a half-smile on her face, she turned to Paddy. "Would you be drinking a cuppa?"

"Tea?" He was embarrassed. To come to grips with the initial situation had cost him emotional effort. He was trying to readjust from an iron determination to an agreeable state of mind. He had never been alone with a woman to sit down to tea. Always there had been someone else, a third party. He thought first of saying, "No, thank you," and starting for home, but there was something so sad about her, that made him want to shake her into happiness.

"That would be grand," he said, and looked around for a spot where he could sit.

She sensed his dilemma. "Over by the fire," she said, "Can ye stir it?"

That he understood, and he leaped to the task. From a pile of turf heaped under the caravan, he seized some clods, and, stirring the embers, raised the glow, and arranged a triangle of turf and fanned the flames with his cap. The turf took the draft and the flames rose, brisk and reassuring. Jane had stepped into the caravan and emerged with a battered metal teapot, a canister of tea and a spoon. Paddy found the copper kettle quite full of water and still hot. It soon boiled. He sat atop the extra turf he had brought over and watched her as she poured water from the kettle into the pot and placed it right in the flames. Soon she took it out and poured them each a cup of tea. She then shook and spread her blanket and sat on it. When she shook the blanket, Paddy once again caught the unpleasant odor. Rain began to fall ever so slightly, causing them to look at each other and smile. She had a lovely smile, he thought, and wondered about her blind eye.

"Would ye be having milk?"

"I would not. Just the tea. The way it is."

She poured milk into her own.

"Did your Da make the kettle?"

"He did," she said, "and many the like of it."

She had the soft Irish speech that his mother had long lost, and he listened contentedly without really following the train of her account of her father's gift with crafts. He did not know whether the rain had stopped or not. He knew simply that he was in no hurry to go home.

8

DR. OLIVE O'BRIEN, short, stout and ebullient, swung her swivel chair to face Father Curtin. Her face was round, more cherubic than chubby, with large laughing blue eyes under typically Celtic salt-and-pepper hair, parted in the middle and falling on either side of her head just below the ears. She was clad in a pink suit, in all ways a sharp contrast to the tall, thin, angular priest in his black clerical clothes, his lined face and coal black thinning hair.

"Come, Father," she said in her broad Donegal accent, which he knew she was intent on retaining, "it's certainly not the first time someone has confessed incest—and to you." He picked up a small jar of capsules from her desk.

"This is quite different," he said with his precise speech. "This was not told me under seal of confession."

"It's been around a long time," she said. "Do you know my famous poem entitled, 'The Children of Cain?'"

The priest cast his eyes to the ceiling.

"When obsessed
"And put to the test,

"They made the best
"Of incest."

"Doctor," he said, "no one appreciates your unrelenting ribaldry more than I, and please don't get into your harangue on *Finnegans Wake*. This is too serious and we're going to do something about it."

She smiled at him and shifted forward in her chair as if in consultation.

"Did I catch a 'we' buried in that last sentence?"

"You did."

"And what is it we're going to be doing?"

"Olive, we're going to take her into your home until we can get her placed working at the hospital in Killarney or cleaning rooms at the Great Southern in Parknasilla."

"Hiring a tinker girl to clean is a new thought in this tired world."

"Oh, I know, God help her. She smells like a barnyard. When I took her in my arms, I would have been sickened by the odor if I had not been overwhelmed with pity. God alone knows what the state of her health is. She tells me a doctor saw her eye. Well, that's your department." He paused. "But I'll tell you this about her soul. It has all the fragrance of innocence and the stuff of sanctity. I shudder when I think of her going back to that brute."

"You sent her back?"

"I couldn't stop her. I honestly think she's more afraid of leaving that way of life, leaving the caravan and the dog, and the road, than she is of his beatings. To come into our world holds more terrors for her than the rigors and the sexual abuse she endures."

"It's a criminal offense, of course. But they never testify against their das."

"I'm sure she wouldn't. She's never known any kindness since her mother died, and when I gave her the money she was trying to steal, it drove her off her head. For a moment, she broke out of her imprisonment and reached in a rush for a different world. It was momentary. Then the fear surged back." He looked pensively at the floor.

The doctor spoke: "Do we kidnap her? Threaten him? Get the Gardai? Who's around? Sergeant Callaghan?"

"She might be induced to run away," he said. "She wants to. She yearns to. Torn between terrors. I told her she had the right to run away. I told her she had the right and duty to resist him, to drive him off, to fight back. She's a strong girl."

"Perhaps one of the decent tinker families would take her in?"

"That's a possibility. I suspect that Ward, from what she told me—that's her father—is an outcast; that the other tinkers, the traveling people, will have nothing to do with him; that they know about his degeneracy. Beating the girl wouldn't turn the others against him. Yet she told me that he's not welcome at any of the gatherings. It makes her isolation all the worse."

"She's gone back to him?"

"She has."

"I hope he doesn't kill her."

"God forgive me, I thought of that."

"Now here, Father, let's get practical. First, we must get her in here, examine her, clean her up, and see what she might want to do. Why don't we go out there together and face him and bring her in. Agreed?"

"That may be best. 'The health board wants her examined.'"

"I am the health board."

"Do we need the Gardai?"

"I don't think so."

"I'll bring my blackthorn. Those rogues are all cowards."

She put on a white knitted hat and a short brown coat and picked up her black bag. "This will impress them," she said.

He had donned his hat. "I have my car," he said, "and my stick's in it."

As they went out the door into the street, Dr. O'Brien said, "Suppose you had been told this in the confessional?"

He paused on the pavement beside the sedan. "My advice would have been the same, but I would have been unable to come to you. Still, I might have been able to persuade her to."

When they were seated, he said, "Faith, you know more secrets than I do." They both laughed.

"They can be burdensome," she said softly.

They drove along in silence until they topped the hill and started the descent past Sullivan's farm with the Madigan house in the distance to the left, a plume of blue smoke ascending from the chimney.

"Sure, there's no wind at all," he said, "but they say the rain will be on us tonight."

Ahead of them, on the slight slope on the right hand side of the road stood the caravan, rather gay in the sunlight despite the peeling paint. The roan horse grazed nearby and the dog slept beside the remains of a fire.

They weren't ten feet from the caravan when the rear door opened and Ward emerged. He had on a brown jacket and trousers, baggy but clean, and a clean white shirt open at his massive throat. His dark hair was slickly combed, parted in the middle and shining. His blue eyes were glassy but sharp. He jumped down from the steps with the agility of a much younger man, and coming toward the priest he crossed himself, bending his right arm with a jerky motion.

"Dia dhuit," he said.

Father Curtin looked at him with a cold eye. "Dia agus Mhuire dhuit," he replied.

The glassy eyes shifted to the doctor standing with her black bag to the rear of the priest. Father Curtin spoke again in Irish, "Where's your daughter?"

The man's face went blank. "I don't have the Irish," he said.

"I didn't think you had," said Father Curtin. "I asked to see your daughter."

"Oh achone," he cried, "there is my heartache. The child has run way."

Father Curtin twisted his head to look at Dr. O'Brien.

"When did she leave?" Dr. O'Brien asked. "We want her for the health board."

"She came back yesterday afternoon and defied me, and when my back was turned, she stole my papers from the caravan and ran off."

"Well she might," said Father Curtin in his exasperation, "the father you've been to her."

"The father I've been to her!" Ward's voice rose in indignation. "Didn't I teach her to cook and to sew? Haven't I fed and clothed her and taught her all the child knows? Betimes I've cared for her and her sick and doctored her! Oho! What better father could she have had?"

The man warmed to his theme. His boldness startled both priest and doctor, and they watched with concealed surprise as he danced about in his verbosity.

"Me, who could jump over that horse there. Given a

pole I could vault the caravan. Who was there was faster in the sprint or could run as far? I could catch a stoat with my bare hands, and taught her to. I can dig you a ditch or build a wall. When the rheumatism wasn't bothering me I could dance you a dance and play on the tin whistle at the same time. I taught her songs but she's slow to learn. You can't trust her, the poor thing—what she says to you, I mean. Sometimes I think she's not right in the head. I have a second sight that way. I can tell you the mare is sick before she heaves. And her mother, the children's mother, I saw her death coming. Just as I seen ye coming today. Why else would I be ready to greet ye with an Irish phrase and my best clothes and all?"

"Ward," said Father Curtin coldly, "you are a liar and a cheat. Where is the girl?"

"You torture me with your doubts. Look in the caravan yerself. She's gone, she's gone, and not able to survive on the roads by herself. A poor unfortunate."

Dr. O'Brien was already checking the interior of the caravan. Father Curtin stood staring at the ground.

"Are ye satisfied now?" Ward asked as the doctor returned.

"She's not there," she said to the priest.

Ward thrust out an accusing finger at Father Curtin. "T'is yerself that did it. T'was ye that she quoted to me. To defy me and, God forgive her, strike me, her own da that's cared for her all these years. Ye'll answer to the High King of Heaven for that. Turning a daughter against her own father. Priest or no priest, I should knock you down."

Throughout the tirade, Father Curtin stood impassive, his cold eyes fixed on the raging man.

"Ward," he said without moving, his blackthorn cane

straight beside him, "you so much as raise your hand and I will not only knock you down, I well see that you spend five years in Port Laois. Is that clear to your sodden mind?"

The tinker ran a hand over his mouth and chin. "Ah, yew misunderstand me," he said. "It's only that that loss of me daughter has sickened my mind. It's the mysterious pull of things in there"—he touched his head with a forefinger—"tells me she's dead, or God knows, worse."

"There is no worse that can happen to her than you've done," said Dr. O'Brien, inserting herself into the exchange.

"Who are you to rag me?"

"I'm the one who knows what you are."

"Are you going to listen to a daft girl? Christ knows what delusions she has. She's tortured me with her nonsense. Go find her. You can have her. She's not fit to beg."

"Ward," said Father Curtin, as coldly as before, "you have heard what I said. Now I will add to that. If you lay one hand again on that girl in anger, punishment or affection—affection—I will have you in Port Laois." He turned on his heel and, hardly waiting for Dr. O'Brien to follow, started down the hill. As they got into the sedan, he said, "I couldn't be civil to him, but who will forgive me if she's dead?"

"That bastard," said Dr. O'Brien, settling back in her seat, "could have killed her, but I don't think he did."

"You restore my hopes," said Father Curtin. "Olive, she has to be alive."

"By God," she said, "he's a superman. I don't doubt a word of his brag. He'll shoe a horse, make a kettle, grow roses, or fight another tinker into the ground; gouge out an eye and drink the crowd out of their wits before he loses his own. The size of him!"

"Once upon a time, maybe," said Father Curtin, "but his

liver can't take much more or I miss my guess. Superman, yes. You remember your Nietzsche?"

"Have you a good quote?"

"'Though goest to woman? Forget not the whip.'"

"That's Nietzsche?"

"Yes, and Mike Ward. But where is she?"

9

PADDY CAME TO the stone pier early in the morning with his fishing pole, hooks, line and a battered can holding bait. Cloud cover, flat, gray and uniform, hid the sky—not the usual scurry of turbulent clouds moving before the west wind. The day was calm, the water dark. It was the sort of day he liked best for fishing: and he was pleased. The sense of pleasure rode in tandem with an excitement he had not felt before, a strange exhilaration that trembled before the possibility of disappointment. She might not come. He did not settle down to his work directly because of his emotion but placed his tackle where he planned to sit and then wandered about the cindery surface of the pier, staring down for a while at a blue and orange launch tied to a rusty ring and an iron bollard. Near the threshold of the pier was a wrecked and stripped automobile body abandoned when its last hour had come and then plundered of all usable parts. He had never known whose it had been. Someday he would have a boat and an automobile. First he would have a bicycle.

The thought came to him that he had often had before. What did his mother do with the money from the farm, from the milk, from her pension, all paid to her directly? Money he was never allowed to handle. When Mulcahy sold the bullocks, the check had been sent to her and as usual she complained that Mulcahy the Thief was cheating her. For a long time he had thought that Mulcahy was a thief and cheating her, but then he learned from hearing people talk in town that Mulcahy was an honest man and was the only one in town who would deal with "that Mrs. Madigan." She gave Paddy two pounds a week for himself. Little enough, he thought. You could spend it in an evening with the price of a pint what it was. When he asked her for more he merely brought on a tirade, a denunciation of the Pope and priests and even the figure of the mother of Christ in a way so blasphemous it terrified him. He was near to having his bicycle by saving. He would ask her again for the extra. He felt a fool always being on foot.

"A bicycle," she had said, "sure, then I'd never see you."

"I could get home faster," he said. She only wagged her head.

Once when he asked her about money and the income from the farm and pressed her, she had fallen in a faint or a fit and he had shaken so in terror that he almost fell himself getting water to revive her.

He looked down the path several times in his anxious waiting and felt a heartache telling him that Jane was not coming. He turned his mind to baiting his hook, and studying the waters before him. A step on the high gravel interrupted his thoughts, and he felt his heart leap. He turned to see Jane descending, smiling and waving, her fishing tackle in her hands.

"Good morning to you," he called.

"Good morning," she said shyly. She wasn't wearing her plaid blanket, so distinctive of tinker women, but a man's raincoat, and her red hair had been neatly bound with a yellow ribbon in a bun on the top of her head. Her smile made him smile, and he reached up a hand to help her down from the walk. They spoke of the weather, and of fish and bait, and then they sat in the silence so beloved of anglers. Nature seemed to speak for them. The solidity of the gray granite pier beneath them, the whispering sea before them, the almost imperceptible movement of the chocolate seaweed in the water and at its edge, sparkling with gold where the light struck, the world of cloud above them, and the palpable absence of wind. Paddy was very conscious that they were sharing it all. The black-capped gulls wheeled above them and he watched with warm attention a flight of curlews that had caught her eye. Without moving her fishing rod, she rolled her head to watch the birds go by. To their astonishment, in that stillness, the great gray heron flapped in on its broad wings and alighted about ten feet from them only to discover their still presence. With a frightened squawking it took off immediately and sailed, like something prehistoric, back along the steep banks of the rocky cove.

"Squawk! Squawk! Squawk!" Jane mocked the cry of the bird and set them both laughing aloud.

"You could bring him back with that cry," Paddy said, and they laughed again.

A duped fish took their attention and they added it to the catch. It came out of the water writhing, and Paddy saw it as a golden thing from another life in another world that was not so far away after all. He slowly came to feel himself the pulsing center of a huge disk of serenity which cast its spell over the sunless waters of the Kenmare River in one direction and over the ranks of hills and mountains in the other. He had never before sensed such a placidity. He knew it had no relation to anything that had been spoken between them. They had been sitting in a prolonged silence when he first became conscious of the sensation which he could not describe to himself clearly and would not dare attempt to describe to anyone else or even mention for fear of embarrassment. But it was as real as the shining fish in the battered can—something he could not analyze, but which had everything to do with the woman sitting beside him.

How different was his reaction to her presence compared to his reaction to the person of Bessie Thompson. Here was no secret terror, no prickly feeling of inferiority, no sad sense of inevitable rebuff. Also there was no sense of adoration, and yet he didn't mean that. Adoration was reserved for Christ, veneration for his Blessed Mother. He struggled to recall the exact words of his catechism but they evaded him.

"Venerate" was not the word for Bessie Thompson. He idolized her—yes, that was it. His imagination pictured her leaving the automobile in which she returned each day from college, and he saw the swirl of her skirt, her smooth nylon-stockinged leg, her hand waving to the driver, and her quick step to her door, the high forehead, the curls, the pink and creamy skin.

He recalled his bumbling effort to talk to her, to invite her out, and for the first time, he understood the sense of misplacement, of broken parts that didn't fit and couldn't fit and couldn't be brought together. Another fish had his line and he quickly hauled it in. When it was landed the picture of Bessie Thompson had gone from his mind, and he was again aware of the disk of serenity. In the distance on the far bank of the sweeping estuary the sun had come through, the west wind was picking up and disrupting the flat cloud cover, the whole sky above them began to move and the rain came.

"Quick!" he said, and they scrambled together to the stripped sedan and crawled inside, thankful for its protective roof.

"I'll clean your fish for you," he said, unsnapping the blade of his knife.

"Good," she said, and smiled as she watched him in the cramped quarters, working on the top of the upended pail, while the rain in its wrath shattered about them.

"This rain won't last long," she said. "You'll have to be getting back."

"And yourself?"

She didn't answer but sat watching him work.

In fifteen minutes the rain had gone, and the sunshine that had begun on the far shore moved across the water, turning it from black to blue, and at length reached the pier. They crawled out of the sedan, brushed off their clothes and without speaking walked off the pier together, Paddy carrying all the fishing tackle and the pail of fish. He noticed that she had paused long enough to throw the gurry into the tide, which he felt he should have done.

As they mounted the slope to the road, he began to talk to her casually about his chores on the farm and to tell her about the cows and the bullocks they had sold and the others they were fattening in their pasture. He began to enjoy a verbosity he had never allowed himself before, careless of whether he sounded the fool or not. He was conscious that she listened to him with close attention, rarely speaking and then using only one word to have him repeat a phrase or further explicate some aspect of his work. He thought to himself in the telling that much of it must have been new to her, to anyone who spent a lifetime on the road.

They had walked along about a quarter of a mile and were approaching the turn into the boreen that led to his home when he found himself curious about her daily life in the caravan and on the roads moving about the country, back and forth, begging for a living, or having her father buy and sell horses or manage some tin work at one farm or another. When Paddy mentioned it at last, she turned toward him with her head down, and said quietly, "I ain't going back."

He was puzzled how to respond to this remark when out of the corner of his eye he caught a flash of gray cloth and to his astonishment saw his mother charging at them from behind a clump of shiny holly trees, her cane wielded above her head.

"Get out of here, ye stinkin' whore!" she screamed as she struck savagely at Jane.

Twice the cane struck the girl on the head before Paddy recovered from his surprise and seized it in his right hand, striving to wrench it from his mother, and pushed her away with his left hand. Jane had fallen against an embankment. He was astounded at his mother's strength and it was several minutes before he could wrench the cane from her grasp, and in his anger fling it far to the left toward some bogland. Throughout the struggle his mother's whine had risen in one profane denunciation after another. He bore through it all, shouting only, "Ma, stop it, for God's sake. Stop!"

At length the panting woman, her weapon taken from her, ceased her turmoil and turned her invective against her son. "What sort of an animal are ye, consortin' with tinker whores?"

Her face was purple with wrath; her lips protruded and

twitched. Her dress had torn at the throat in the struggle, but her hair, braided and coiled, was still tight on her head. Her green eyes glared above the dirty wrinkles of her face. His chest heaving—not so much from the exertion as from his emotion of mingled rage, disgust and shock—Paddy turned to Jane, only to find that she had disappeared. He was stunned by her absence.

She couldn't have run up the road or she would surely still be in sight. He sprang to the top of the embankment against which she had fallen, broke through a cluster of bushes and surveyed the bogland before him. She could have been concealed in half a dozen places, yet it didn't seem possible. It had all happened so quickly.

"Jane! Jane!" he called again and again, walking slowly and looking left and right. "For God's sake, Jane, come back, come back!"

No answer came. Some curlews flew above him with their soft sad call, and far off rooks were cawing. In the stillness, he could hear the gurgle of the brook. With terror in his heart he ran toward it, slipping occasionally in the muck but righting himself quickly. When he got to the brookside, he had to walk into the middle up to his hips in the water in order to see both up and down the muddy stream, its roiling water yellow with foam at the banks. Satisfied she was not in the brook, he turned back to the boreen where his mother had caned her. His fishing tackle, the pail and the fish were scattered on the road where he had flung them. Racked with his conflicting emotions, he gathered up the gear, put the cleaned and uncleaned fish back in the pail, now emptied of its water, and started for home.

When he entered the house, he found that his mother had locked herself in her bedroom. He put the fish in water in the sink, washed his hands, and stood in dumb wonder about what to do.

"That was a terrible thing you did," he shouted at her door. "You're a dreadful woman!" The imprecation was the worst he had ever put on her.

A prayer rose in his throat as he ran out the door and along the boreen to the main road, careless of his wet clothes. He must get to the caravan. As he started along, the rain began again, but he was not conscious of it. All the way to the main road and the caravan he kept watching the countryside for a sign of the girl. Several times he called out her name, but only more bird cries mocked his anguish.

Ward was entering the caravan when Paddy reached the bottom of the slope.

"Where's Jane?" he called.

"Who are ye?"

"I'm a friend."

"Then ye tell me where she is. She left here last night and didna return."

"Last night? She wasn't here last night?"

"That's what I said."

The man turned his back and went into the caravan, leaving Paddy baffled and frightened. He was about to leave when the plaid blanket she usually wore sailed out of the rear of the caravan and landed ten strides from him, crumpled in the grass. He paused a moment and then stepped forward and picked it up, looking across at the caravan. He half expected something to be said, but the car doors closed. The dreadful barnyard odor came from the blanket and he was about to throw it on the ground, when he decided to take it with him to wash and have ready for her return. He went homeward dreading the sight of his mother and trying to recall his last image of Jane. He could see only the cane descending twice rapidly and he could hear the sound of the blows, and his mother's screaming vituperation. He tried to remember if he had seen blood on Jane's forehead Fearing she might be unconscious in the fields, he wandered for an hour searching but found no trace of her. He returned home sick from despondency.

His mother was again sitting by the stove darning socks, her arthritic, swollen hands moving like claws. He remembered the strength in them and guessed how hard the blows on Jane's head must have been. Looking at his mother, he felt welling up in him a detestation he had never known before. But he had nothing to add to what he had already said. He said it again, with added intensity: "You are a dreadful woman!"

He could not bring himself to eat the supper she put before him, but left the house and walked the countryside again, his collie with him, finding nothing but his mother's cane. He carried it part of the way home and then, reexamining it for blood stains, he threw it in the brook. It told him nothing, but he felt contaminated holding it. When he closed the door of his room that night, he could not sleep. He was lying on his bed, praying, his mind churning, when his mother shouted through the door: "You'll live to thank me one day."

In a rage that blinded him, he sprang from his bed and ran toward the door. But he stopped with his right hand on the handle, and put his head against the door, weeping into his other hand. For half an hour he stood there. Then he turned and lay down again. He felt somehow only half a man. He had to talk to someone.

He resolved to appeal to Father Curtin the next day, and to tell him all that had happened.

10

THE MASS WAS at six o'clock and always, Paddy knew, Father Curtin was the celebrant. Paddy was the first person to enter the church and the last to leave. He went directly to the sanctuary and stood watching the priest divest himself of his chasuble, cincture and alb, pulling the last garment over his head. Timidly, Paddy coughed to announce his presence and nodded in response to the priest's greeting.

"I have to talk to you, Father," he said.

"Come in, Paddy, come in. What is it?"

"It's the tinker girl, Father."

He halted and trembled and then a floodgate within him let go, and he heard himself, as if in someone else's voice, recounting for the priest all that had happened, sensing the mingled anger and anxiety in his story. He had often felt like a fool in the past but never more so than now. He was aware that he disclosed more affection for the tinker girl than he thought he had, and he burned with shame for his mother and still more for the despise he felt for her in his heart.

"And that's a true account, is it, Paddy?" the priest asked. "You have left nothing out?"

"As God and Mary are my witness, Father."

"And this was Thursday?"

"It was, Father, Thursday." Noticing a look of doubt on the priest's face, he was prompted to say: "Why do you ask me again?"

"Because, Paddy," the priest said slowly and reflectively, "Dr. O' Brien and I visited Mr. Ward that very day and he told us she had run away the night before."

"He told me that, too," said Paddy, blushing at the priest's implication that he had not been truthful. He then added, "I don't know where she spent the night."

"We were afraid he might have harmed her," Father Curtin said, "but if you were with her the next day, he couldn't have."

"It was my mother that hurt her," Paddy said bitterly. He was unable to restrain his tears.

"Come, come, Paddy," the priest said, putting a hand on his bowed head, "we'll find her. But first we must see the Gardai."

Together they left the church and made their way to the Siochana. It all seemed to Paddy like a dream. Somewhere far away from him, he saw the circle of contentment, a vast and shining disc in the center of which he had stood for an hour, another world from the world he lived in, an illumination that he somehow associated with growth. Then he saw a disfigurement disrupt it: his mother's slashing cane, her obscene cries, and the whole illumination rolled up like a torn window shade, with a snap. They arrived at the Siochana just as Sergeant Callaghan was opening the door for the day.

The sergeant was a large man, with a curled black

mustache, red cheeks and blonde hair parted in the middle and curling violently despite obvious efforts to slick it down. When he sat behind his desk he looked a man of forty, but Paddy knew they were of an age. Paddy had often wondered if the mustache was dyed and when the thought came to him now he dismissed it as unworthy. There were times when to think ill of someone seemed to hurt him physically, a trait that made the image of his mother in his heart so galling. It rocked within him like a jagged stone.

"We've come to report the tinker girl, Jane Ward, missing, Sergeant," Father Curtin said. The sergeant pushed some papers about on the top of his desk, and Paddy surmised that he was merely giving himself time to think.

"I'm not sure, Father," Callaghan said, "that it's proper for me to record the girl as a missing person when her own father has not so reported her."

"He tells me she has run away," the priest replied.

The sergeant again deliberated. "He could be lying to you to put you off."

"He could, and indeed I think he would lie quite readily. But I don't think he is lying. The girl is missing and Dr. O'Brien shares my concern for her, and I think when you hear Paddy's story, you'll find a course of action before you."

The sergeant looked steadily at Paddy. Paddy knew that his respect for authority turned to fright when any garda confronted him, even if the man was his equal in age. He was for the moment quite unable to speak. His hands tugged at his cap as if he had no control of them, and although he wet his lips half a dozen times, he still stood silent.

"Tell him, Paddy," the priest prompted, "just what you told me."

Unable to keep a tremor from his voice, Paddy

struggled through the story, including his visit to the caravan and Mike Ward. When he finished the sergeant continued making notes on a pad before him, and then tapped the pad with his pencil for a while before speaking. "Whatever else has happened here," he said, "it seems certain there's been an assault."

"By my mother," said Paddy, swallowing so that the words were almost indistinguishable.

"Just so," said the sergeant. "Now then, although we can understand your mother's outrage seeing you with the tinker lass, she's guilty of assault and liable to arrest. It's not like the father beating the girl. We all know about that."

His voice rambled on ponderously, but Paddy had begun to shake at the contempt that attended the sergeant's phrase, "seeing you with the tinker lass." He knew it was the way his mother felt. But they were wrong. They didn't know Jane as he did. He was trying in his mind to frame a response to the insinuation when Father Curtin interrupted the sergeant's discourse.

"Let me make a point, if I may, sergeant," he said in an incisive tone. "I think we can both agree that Paddy is telling the truth. The mother's assault was unwarranted. But where did the girl go? If she went back to the caravan, her father might well have killed her. He is a violent, dangerous and powerful man whose moods, from drink, are out of control. I think before we lose time talking to Mrs. Madigan, we had best confront Mike Ward. We must remember that at the moment there is no one to press charges against Mrs. Madigan. That is why I say that, at bottom, this case is the case of a missing person—perhaps a victim of murder."

"Oh, my God," Paddy groaned, and leaned against the sergeant's desk for support.

Driving out to the caravan, Paddy slumped in the back

seat of the police car, locked in a stupor of pain and nameless fright. His benumbed mind tried to sort out the course of his fears. He was not afraid of Mike Ward, nor of physical violence. He was afraid for his mother that she would be arrested. He was timid before the ponderous authority of Sergeant Callaghan. He was ashamed before Father Curtin for the actions of his mother. But in his heart—what made it shrink and throb—he knew that he was afraid for Jane, afraid that his mother had injured her badly, afraid that her drunken father might have killed her after all, afraid that she had fled Kerry forever, afraid that he had lost her before he ever possessed her. It was when he stood in the sanctuary telling the story to the priest that he had recognized in the depth of his being his love for Jane.

He laid his cheek against the cool leather of the rear seat and again felt a sense of nausea. He yearned to hear her voice; he ached to see her. He wanted to leave the automobile and run to wherever she might be, and then he recognized his deepest terrors: his mother's blows might have killed her. He only half heard the conversation between the priest and the garda in the front seat. It implied something about the girl and her father that he didn't want to hear, that his soul rejected as soon as he had half grasped it, and he determined in his heart that he hadn't heard it. It had been whispered and he was able to dismiss it as a dream. He banished it from his thoughts. Suddenly, he sat up and grasped the priest by the shoulder.

"She's alive!" he said. "She has to be alive."

They had arrived at the slope where the caravan rested. Father Curtin looked back at him, the reflection of light on his spectacles hiding whatever might have shown in his eyes.

"Do not agitate youself, Paddy," he said. "I understand.

We'll find her."

The sergeant parked the car by the side of the road and turned to Father Curtin. "I think, Father, if you don't mind, Paddy and I will go up together. It's not that you are . . ."

Father Curtin raised a deprecatory hand. "I understand perfectly, sergeant," he said. "I'm here simply to help. If I am needed, call me. Go with him, Paddy."

Together, Paddy and the sergeant mounted the slope. Even as they came up the incline, they could see Ward, and Paddy could tell by the man's posture as he leaned against the caravan that he was drunk. Paddy stood a respectful distance behind the sergeant, who addressed the tinker: "Is your name Mike Ward?"

"It is that. True for you." The words gurgled out of the man's throat.

"I am given to understand that your daughter is missing."

"Lured away by that fucking priest."

Paddy hunched his shoulders as if he were chilled.

"I'll thank you to mind your language when you're talking to me."

"She's gone right enough."

"You have no thought as to where?"

"I have not."

"Or who she might have gone with?"

Ward started to move away from the side of the caravan but almost lost his balance and quickly fell back. His speech became so slurred that it was difficult to understand him. He ran his hand over his mouth as if to help him repeat his words, and with a sudden gesture hitched up his sagging trousers and resettled the battered felt hat on his head. "Why don't you ask that simple-minded bastard behind you?"

Paddy, despite his funk, bristled. He would have

spoken, but the sergeant was before him. "What's he got to do with it?"

"He was here yesterday and stole her blanket."

The sergeant beckoned Paddy up beside him. "Is that true?"

"He threw it out," said Paddy. "I took it and washed it. It's hanging on my line."

The tinker threw back his head and laughed. "Woman's work!" he sneered.

"Ward," said the officer, "I'm going to report your daughter missing."

"S'all right."

"If she comes back, notify us. Understand?"

Ward nodded.

"And as soon as she does," the sergeant said, a touch of menace coming into his voice, "you and the bitch get out of this town. Is that clear?"

The tinker's lips framed an obscenity but no sound came. Paddy watched the sergeant walk to the rear of the caravan and look inside. He felt a detestation for the man. The word "bitch" rang in his ears like an alarm bell. He wanted to fight, to strike somebody, something, to take the circumstances that surrounded him and crush them in his hands. He had never known such emotion before and he was afraid of it, afraid of himself. With an effort, he went up to the sergeant, who, having finished his inspection of the interior of the caravan, was walking back toward the sedan.

"Sergeant!" cried Paddy. "Sergeant!"

The sergeant kept walking but turned his head over his shoulder to look at Paddy.

"You can't call that woman a 'bitch.' You can't."

"Aw, Christ, I didn't mean to," the sergeant replied.

"It's just that I hate that bastard so. He was a great athlete in his day, tinker or not, a champion at any feis. Ruined by the drink. I'd like to wring his neck. Put his face in the muck and drown him."

"She's a good woman," Paddy said.

"I'm sure. I'm sure. I'm sorry," the sergeant muttered. "Let's go see your mother."

As they approached the police car, Paddy saw the priest leaning against it with his arms folded on his chest. Sergeant Callaghan looked at the priest, nodded his head toward the caravan behind him, and then shook his head from side to side and looked at the ground.

"He's too drunk to tell us what he knows," he said, "but he acknowledges the lass is missing. I'll call for a search." While Paddy and the priest stood by, the sergeant informed his headquarters on the radio of the girl's disappearence and gave a description. "She's not much of a looker," he said. "Five foot four in height, red hair, broken nose and a bad left eye. Typical broad tinker face."

Paddy tapped him on the arm. "She has a lovely smile," he said and paused. The officer took the transmitter away from his mouth and stared down at him. Paddy flushed and raised his right hand to point to his own mouth. "Very even teeth," he said. "She has very even teeth."

"She has very even teeth," the sergeant repeated into the microphone. He turned to Paddy. "What was she wearing when you saw her?"

"A raincoat—a light brown raincoat—and a cotton dress."

"That's it?"

Paddy nodded. His sense of inadequacy stirred him. At length, the sergeant turned away from the radio. "They'll mount a search," he said. "I'll have a chat with your mother."

They drove from the slope down to the boreen that led to the Madigan farm, the brilliant sunshine contrasting with Paddy's mental blackness.

"This time I'll ask the two of you to remain behind," the garda said, turning his red face round on them. Paddy was relieved not to have to go in.

"I'll wait until he comes out and then go in," he said, abstractedly. "I' m not happy here—I mean, there."

Father Curtin turned to look at him and Paddy could read compassion in his face.

"I think now I was never happy there," Paddy said. He buried his face in his hands, and did not move until the sergeant returned. He felt the priest's hand on his shoulder and found it impossible to look up at him.

"As soon as we hear something," Father Curtin said, "I'll come out and let you know. Pray, Paddy, say your prayers. Prayer can help everyone, including her. They'll find her."

After they had gone, he went into the vegetable garden, where he could kneel unchallenged amid the rows of cabbages and beans. Tomorrow, he told himself, I'll comb the hills for her myself.

11

ALL DAY SATURDAY Paddy walked the bogs and the mountains behind the caravan and along the banks of the brook, searching for the slightest clue, struggling to hope.

Late in the afternoon he recovered from the brook the cane his mother had used to strike Jane, but again it told him nothing. At home he found himself unable to speak to his mother no matter how she badgered him. The passage of time was interminable, the hours were a torment. The night was sleepless and he would have run all the way to early mass on Sunday if Mrs. Mulcahy had not stopped to offer him a ride.

"You're early, Paddy, and so am I for a change. It's a fortuitous meeting."

The word "fortuitous" was new to him but be immediately linked it with "fortune" in his head, with "luck" and with "chance" and then "misfortune," for his mind now ran always to gloom.

"I'm very grateful," he said, stumbling over the words because of the turmoil in his mind.

"I see the helicopter over the mountains," Mrs. Mulcahy

said, obviously unaware of his distress. "They're looking for that Ward girl. It was on the wireless."

"I know," said Paddy. He came close to telling her the whole story. It had been an agony to live Saturday without speaking of the matter to his mother, to somebody. He too had heard the radio report, which had not mentioned either his connection with the case or his mother's. "I hope they find her," he managed to say.

"They say in town her father treated her something dreadful. Maybe she did away with herself."

"She wouldn't do that," Paddy cried impulsively, causing the woman to turn and look at him. "I don't think of a young woman doing that," he added lamely. He was relieved when he was able to leave the automobile and hurry into the church, almost sprinting up the street.

The curate offered the mass and called for prayers from the congregation that the tinker girl might be found. The announcment read from the altar just before the Gospel revealed only that the girl's father had reported to the Gardai that she was missing. But as the congregation left the church, Paddy could overhear conversations and chance remarks exchanged by the parishioners. Almost all indicated that the sooner she was found the sooner would the drunken tinker and his disgraceful caravan leave town, and they would no longer have her begging in the streets, an embarrassment to the townsfolk and some of the tourists.

"The town should pay her to stand around. The tourists love to photograph her," one man said laughing. "She's so exquisitely dirty."

The general tone depressed him further. He felt isolated because of his involvement with the case, unable to speak about it.

He remained in town to watch the informal mobilization for the search. The presence of the helicopter over the Reeks, as the mountains were called, and its contact by radio with the police cars provided a lively break in the subdued day-to-day movements of the townspeople. Any number of men and women found time to drive up the mountains to scan the countryside. The Boy Guides, members of the local anglers' club, and commercial fishermen as well, scoured the waterways and shoreline and declared that each individual pier that jutted its granite shelf into the Kenmare River would be checked. Paddy, sick of the conversations in the pubs, walked home with reluctant feet and a heart that ached. Monday he again searched the countryside. Tuesday came and went with no word.

He neglected his farm work and ignored his mother. While she ragged at him and ranted, he was hardly aware of her presence. He moved like a man in a dream, although it was for him a nightmare. The pubs were alive with gossip but he noticed that the conventional wisdom of the bars was altering.

"Sure the snip got tired of the beatings," said Casey to his clique of topers, "hitched a lift to Galway, Cork, or even Dublin, and has gone off on her own. The old man was in here Monday night to buy a drink and I threw him out. He's a powerful bastard. Let him buy a bottle and drink in the van."

Paddy listened, trembling in his determination not to speak up no matter what was said. He stood against a wide wall, lost in the shadows, afraid that the light would reveal his agitation.

"Callaghan has ordered him out of town as soon as the girl is found."

"Should have done that the gray day he came into town,

bedad."

Wednesday, when Paddy started to town, he observed that the caravan was gone from the slope with only some trash and the dead ashes from the fire to mark where Mike Ward had camped. That night in the pub Casey announced that his midweek receipts had been stolen. Paddy was with the line of customers when Casey told the news.

"By God, Casey," one man cried, "he was here after more than a drink the night you gave him the frog march."

"T'was him, all right," Casey responded, "who else? When I threw him out the front door, he must have slunk around to the back. The wife was shopping in Kenmare and me daughters were both at the hooley."

While it was understood that Sergeant Callaghan or some other of the Gardai would overtake Ward on the road, there was little chance of recovering the money, let alone proving that Ward was the thief who slipped into the Casey home and stole the receipts of three days.

"Ah, bad cess to him," said Casey. "I hope he chokes on the money. He's a cute one. He left the checks and the hundred pound notes. He knows we take the numbers on them."

"I think," said a bearded man standing close to Paddy, "that they'll find the lass in the back of the caravan. It was mere diversion to have her missing, and everyone of us rooting around in the hills and foostering about so that more than one house could be looted."

"By God," said a stout woman sitting at one of the tables, "you've hit on something there, Larry. There's more than one of us tonight will look under the mattress to see if the sly hoard is still safe."

The exchange brought a shout from the other customers

and even forced a smile to Casey's lips. The bearded man called Larry spoke again: "That's if the girl's hand was under the mattress when she was taking a ride on the top!" The men at the bar roared.

"He shouldn't say a thing like that!" Paddy expostulated. Two young men nearby looked at him and laughed again. The stout soured in his mouth and he turned from the bar and left. Outside in the purpling twlight, he felt as if he were going to retch. He leaned a hand against the wall of the building, inhaled deeply three times, and started the long walk home. He had grown up in the town with a reputation, he knew, of being an odd lad. But he felt that he knew the people better than they knew him. He now sensed in the talk about the tinkers a different and deeper tone, not of amusement, as it had often been, but of disdain, contempt and worse. It was not his mother alone who shouted, "Tinker whore!"

12

DESPITE THE CYNICAL byplay in the pubs, the search went on. Paddy's share took him up the hills and down the shore, and more than once back to the spot where the caning had taken place. He studied the embankment where Jane had leaned after the blows had fallen and stared over it along the road before him. She couldn't have moved fast enough to have disappeared in that stretch while he grappled with his mother. Then it occurred to him. She must have fled back the way they had come, back toward the pier—back, back, away from the caravan, away from it all. He would find her at the center of the disc of serenity. She would have sensed it that day as well as he, and it must have drawn her, battered and bewildered, back as to a haven.

He ran along the path toward the pier where they had fished, and down the incline, half expecting to find her hiding in the skeleton of the abandoned automobile. Oh, God, let her be alive! The rusting wreck was empty. He stood on the granite edge of the pier looking down at the blue and orange motor launch and knew that all his flesh and bones, if not his mind, were telling him that he would find her in a boat, for she had spoken of boats as someone might speak of Paradise. At the next pier along the shore lay a derelict dragger. If she had come to this pier and the tide was low, as it had been at that time of day, for it was receding when they had begun their walk back, she could have walked or waded along the shore to the further pier. With the tide high one would have to circle back, past the Madigan farm, down the narrow boreen, even to the main road, and then have a mile walk. The tide was still ebbing now and he felt certain he could make it along the shore, much the shortest route. He jumped into the water and began to wade along. The water was cold and up to his hips. But at least the sea was calm and he moved along beside the shore with its impenetrable, tangled growth.

As he went he found the water shallower and he made more rapid progress. Jesus, Mary and Joseph, he cried, let it not be my mother's blow that killed her. She will be on the dragger; she will be alive! She hadn't taken to the road; she had taken to hiding from despair. The same iron clamps that had caught his soul had caught hers. He knew. He slipped, fell and plunged headlong into the water. Cursing, he staggered upright and swayed on his feet and continued. He came to a stretch of sand where he would sprint for twenty yards only to come to a mass of algae-covered rocks that made his passage tortuous and painful.

At last he all but fell into a stretch of open shore which, when mounted, led him directly to the neighboring pier. He ran down it and faced the derelict dragger.

"Jane!" he called. There was no reply. A kingfisher, an iridescent jewel, its blue feathers flashing an unbelievable brilliance, rose from a nearby perch and flew past him in fright. He leaped from the pier onto the deck of the derelict, slipping and falling against an ugly pile of rusted cable. Why had no one been here before? They must have. They had searched everywhere. The cabin door stood aslant on its broken hinges, and in his near demented eagerness, he wrenched it from them and threw it onto the deck.

She lay in her brown raincoat, black and wet and disheveled, on a bench at the side of the cabin where no one might have seen her had they not moved the door. Her red hair fell over her face like a veil, but not thickly enough to hide the dark maroon patch of dried blood on her forehead. He fell on his knees beside her, and brushed the hair aside. He leaned over and kissed the clotted wound.

"Jane," he cried, "oh, my God, speak to me!" He turned her head in his hands until the smudged face looked up at him. The blood had run down over her bad eye and her crooked nose, making a mask of horror. Her lips moved but no sound came. He seized her hand, rubbed it and kissed it. She looked at him and half smiled, but her eyes closed and she was limp in his arms. The pier, he knew, was a half mile from the road, and there was probably no house along the shore for half a mile. He climbed back onto the pier, not knowing what he was seeking. A curragh? To row, where? Even if he rowed to his own pier, he would still be a mile from a telephone. He didn't dare try to carry her to the main road. He was afraid to move her from where she lay. He thrust his handkerchief into the sea and went back to the cabin. Tenderly, he wiped the blood from her face, talking all the time.

"Jane, listen to me, mavourneen, listen. Can you hear me?"

Her eyes opened, and then shut again.

"Listen, my love, listen. I have to go and get help. But

you are all right. I've found you. I will take you home. You will be well again. Don't try to move. Wait for me here. Wait. I'll come. I'll come."

He doffed his jacket to cover here, but finding it soaking wet from his fall into the water, he cursed it and threw it down.

"Wait for me. I'll be back. I must get help." He climbed again to the pier, and then jumped back and darted into the cabin. From his right hand, he took his father's ring.

"Can you feel this, Jane? Can you feel it?"

He placed it in the palm of one hand and closed her fingers on it.

"I'll be back."

He fled from the boat to the pier, from the pier to the road—little more than a path that led to the highway.

"Christ have mercy! Christ have mercy!"

The prayer came with each breath. The path seemed interminable but at long last turned out into the highway. He was uncertain which way to run, but unable to remember any house which might have a telephone between this pier road and the Sullivan farm, he turned the other way, running toward Castle Cove. He found a house within two hundred yards, but there was no answer to his knocking. The second house brought a response.

A young boy in bare feet came to the door and stared at Paddy with fear in his eyes.

"I'm wet," Paddy said, "I know. There's been an accident. Tell your mother that I must use the telephone."

The boy cautiously closed the door and left Paddy standing and shaking on the steps. At last, the door reopened and a young blond woman looked at him expectantly.

"I must use your telephone," he said, "I've found the lost girl."

"Lost girl?"

"Please, oh, please just telephone Dr. O'Brien in Sneem and ask her to come here—quick. Say the lost girl is found and she's hurt."

The woman turned without a word and closed the door. Paddy tried to open it but it was locked. He waited, praying.

The woman returned quite soon. "She's coming," she said, and then, "You're wet, and you must be cold. Would you take some tea?"

Too unsettled to say thank you, Paddy shook his head and walked slowly back to the highway and the pier road. He ached to get back to the dragger. He thought of going back to the house and having the woman telephone directions to the pier. He had been stupid. The Bunnow pier, was it? He was not sure of the name. Let it go. Dr. O'Brien would already be out of the house. He sat down with his back against a bank of fuschia that rose behind him like a wall of blood, but his nerves wouldn't let him be still. He rose and paced and prayed and paced some more. When the automobile which he recognized came up the highway, he ran out to greet it, almost bumping into it as it slowed down. He opened the door and jumped in beside Dr. O'Brien.

"Have you told the Gardai?" she asked.

"No! No!," he said. "There is no time. You must see her. Turn about! Turn about! Down to the Bunnow Pier."

Dr. O'Brien swung the automobile around and headed along the main road, taking a right turn at the pier path, an overgrown boreen just broad enough to admit one car.

"She's in the old wreck," he said, "and she's weak. She's been bleeding."

The sedan rolled onto the pier, broad enough to allow it to turn around. Paddy helped Dr. O'Brien down onto the deck and went with her into the cabin and stood by while she made a cursory examination of the stricken woman.

"She can be moved all right, Paddy," she said. "Can you carry her out of here and up to my car?"

He caught the unconscious woman up in his arms and her eyes opened and she looked at him again. Again her lips moved but made no sound. He kissed her forehead, stepped onto the deck and then onto the listing gunnel. To get Jane to the pier, he had to raise her, with great effort, and lay her on the granite blocks almost above his head. While the doctor knelt beside her, he scrambled up and lifting her again, put her into the rear seat of the sedan.

"I'll hold her," he said. "Will she be all right?"

"Let' s get her to my office, Paddy."

He held her tenderly, his left arm couched behind her head and shoulders. Her face looked up into his, and he saw in it, slowly dissipating, the look of a frightened animal—the blue eye at first staring in fear, but then warming gradually, and his heart leaped as it focussed on him. Ever so slowly, Jane's face was transformed and she smiled.

"It's you, Paddy," she said. He nodded, tears near his eyes, and his throat choking.

"You came back," she said.

"I did," he said. "I'm here. You'll be fine, you'll be fine."

He pressed her closely to him and closed his own eyes and waited for the sedan to stop. When it did, he carried her into the small clinic that adjoined the doctor's office.

"Paddy, this girl is close to pneumonia," the doctor said, "and I'm sure she has had a concussion. Tell Mrs. McCann to come immediately, and then go tell the Gardai to call off the search."

As Paddy turned to go, Jane held his hand, and he knew

she was as reluctant to have him go as he was to leave her. Dr. O'Brien took the girl's hand from him and held it in her own. Paddy saw that it was closed tightly on the ring he had pressed on her. He ran down the street to Mrs. McCann's and brought her back with him, and watched them close the door of the clinic.

With mixed emotions, he walked to the Siochana Gardai to report that the girl had been found. An amiable young garda—less intimidating than Sergeant Callaghan—spent an hour taking his statement, interrupting every so often to answer the telephone or a call on the wireless, confirming word that the girl had been found alive.

"Alive," Paddy thought, "but, ah, so sick, so hurt, so abused."

13

AS PADDY LEARNED later, Father Curtin planned the wedding, acting in loco parentis. The priest knew that despite Paddy's earnest desire to marry, and despite his affection for Jane, and despite the girl's trust in Paddy, to bring them together in matrimony would be as difficult as it would have been for someone to get him to abandon his vow of celibacy and run off with a nun. Paddy's terror of his mother was of twenty years' duration, and Jane's fear of any life but that of the roads—the only one she had ever known—was equally rooted in her psyche. He needed an ally to mount his campaign and Dr. O'Brien was the obvious one, perhaps the only one. He made his way from the presbytery to her office with dignity shaken by apprehension.

Dr. Olive O'Brien was the only physician in town, or in the three adjoining towns, and the busiest person in any one of them. He was at length in her office beside the clinic that adjoined the kitchen and the first floor bedroom that had become Jane's home after she had recovered from the drain on her stout constitution caused by the concussion she had received and the days of exposure without sustenance or care. Dr. O'Brien, he noticed, was animated by her usual ebullience.

"The whole thing seems illegal to me," she said. "Yet, I suppose no member of the Irish clergy is concerned with legalities."

"Whether or not it is moral wouldn't concern you, I'm sure," he countered. He leaned back from her cluttered desk and smiled.

"What you plan to do," she said, "is force these two young people—I suppose twenty-two is now considered young in Ireland—against their culturally-induced demurrers into a permanent relationship which will stagger them. Neither one of them is truly equipped."

Father Curtin leaned forward again, his arms on her desk. "You have assured me the young lady is sound in mind and body, and that the young man is also—insofar as he would let you near his person."

"I've given the poor girl a crash course in personal hygiene and high heels," she said, "and she's wearing the first bra and Kotex she's ever seen. Now, despite her hard life, she's a shy, intelligent, sensitive creature and as docile as a jenny. So is he. I trust he will not have the qualms with her he had with me in letting me near his person and his penis."

"Please, doctor," he said, raising his hand, and twisting his smile out of recognition in order to hide it. "Your ribaldry, your candor, your clinical vocabulary. . . I have talked to them both about marriage and I think they know more about it than half the married couples in town."

"Can we be serious for a moment?" she asked, leaning toward him, her Celtic salt-and-pepper hair falling against both temples.

"Heavens," he said, "I dread being serious about it. Do you think I am not aware of the burden I am putting on these young people—and God knows he is young. Of course I do. That girl has never lived under a roof in all her days. She is a nomad; a bedouin. She has no doubt certain talents, but what will be their worth on a farm? He is curiously fastidious; can she be? He is terrified of social stigma and his mother's tongue, and he will have to bear the onus of marrying a tinker who can easily be the butt of obscene jokes. Some of the townsfolk will never let him forget he married a tinker. Oh, they can be charitable and they can be loving, but in a moment of irritation or anger or of malevolence, they will throw it up to him or to her and rake their hearts. The two of them will suffer in the future, but no more than in the past. But this time they will be suffering on the side of life and personal fulfillment."

"What about his mother? They can't possibly live with her."

Father Curtin looked at her wistfully and ran his hand over his thinning hair. "I hadn't told you about that."

"Here it comes!"

"I am quite convinced that the poor woman is demented."

"Do you deem anti-clericalism symptomatic of lunacy?"

"If I didn't have a touch of it myself I might," he said. "Have you tried to examine her?"

"Do you think I'm demented?"

"I see. Well, there you have it. We can be sure that the minute he tells her that he is going to marry—marry anyone—she will throw him out of the house."

"Can she do that?"

"All the legalities are on her side. I don't know whether I can steel him to tell her. He is so incensed over the assault on Jane that his outrage should strengthen his will. The whole episode—the assault, the rescue, his finding her, all that—has moved him profoundly. I don't think he knew he loved her until that day. Olive, as you say, he is not unintelligent; it is simply that he has been deprived, emotionally and in a hundred other ways. That's all. We have them, each without a home. Her father has fled; his mother will reject him. He can't grow into full manhood until he gets out of that house. They must find a temporary place until they find a home."

The doctor looked at him with a full smile on her round, cherubic face, and started to chuckle. He smiled back. "You are not unintelligent yourself," he said, looking up at the ceiling. "You know what's coming."

"God help me," she said, "I do. If I were your wife, I could stop this nonsense by threatening to leave you. You manage to look sufficiently forbidding to hide that mushy heart of yours."

"I prefer to think of it as a very sensible heart," he replied. "Consider how we are helping the world. First, the man is aching to be married. Better, St. Paul tells us, to marry than to burn in single unhappiness, and he is burning. He has never known a tender moment in his life. I'll wager on that. Nor has the girl since her mother died. Think what marriage will do for her. She will discover that what has been a horror for her—God knows how many times—can become one of the sweetest exchanges on God's earth. Second, the West of Ireland has too many bachelors. It's our curse. Paddy will find no one else. I don't think there is another girl in town that would have him, perhaps in the county. He's not the preeminent catch. And then, there's that mother of his. That alone. What woman would face it? Poor chap, he tried for the most attractive young lady in town. That shows sensitivity and taste. The girl? What is her future without Paddy? To go back to that bestial father? To beg on the roads by herself? To turn whore in Galway, Dublin or England? Men of vision and wealth in this country try mightily to settle the traveling people into a sedentary and less parasitic way of life. We are helping there. Once they are married, why, then her father will have no more claim on her, and Paddy's first duty will be to her and not to his mother. This is not Japan."

"They are both terrified?"

"They are, of course. Paddy of his mother and the future. The girl of us and our way of life, of the world, of everybody—excepting, I know for sure, Paddy. She trusts him."

"And how will he support her?"

"I've arranged for him to work for Donal Mulcahy and room with Mrs. McCann. Until the wedding."

"And where will they live after the wedding?" She dropped her head to look at him balefully. He sat hoping she might speak again, but she was obviously determined to make him make the request.

"Just until they can find a place of their own!"

"Am I running a hostel for every horny farm hand in Kerry who's afraid of his mother? I had the girl two weeks as a patient, now as a house guest, and now, thanks to you, I'm going to have him as well."

The priest removed his spectacles and wiped them with deliberation. "The wedding will be in the rectory," he said after a pause. "I don't want his mother disrupting the ceremony. We will skip publishing the banns of marriage! It's quite canonical. We'll give the town a fait accompli. God knows, everyone will know soon enough. And, oh yes—thank you, Olive, for everything. The Lord will bless you; as a matter of fact He already has."

He rose to leave and she to usher him out.

"To be very honest about it, Dan," she said, using his first name, which she did only when she was very serious, "I've a great deal more confidence about the success of it than I had when you first spoke. I think they can make it, if the Lord will take the mother and the Gardai will jail her father."

Father Curtin raised both hands in the air. "Something had to be left to God," he said. "You've been glorious in giving." He turned back. "May I make a last request? Will you be a witness? The maid of honor, in a manner of speaking." The eyeglasses twinkled.

She laughed aloud. "I should knock you down."

"Five years in Port Laois," he said and left.

14

THE NIGHT BEFORE the day he told his mother that he was going to marry Jane, Paddy walked the floor almost until the sun rose. Since the assault a month before, they had rarely spoken to each other. While this bothered him when they were in the same room, it was also a relief. He had felt his love for her peel away, and only a sense of obligation remained. He had long been weary of her ranting and her whine. Although he could not put a finger to the nub of it, and had no words to describe it, he was conscious of a deterioration in her. Lest the old relationship begin to seed itself, he had taken to leaving the house whenever she did speak, and he became conscious that she talked more and more to herself when they were in separate rooms. Five times he had been on the brink of saying to her boldly, "Ma, I'm going to marry Jane Ward," but had been unable to bring himself to do so. His night of pacing and praying had stiffened his spine.

It was evening. She had put his supper on the table without a word, and had taken her seat by the stove to resume her interminable knitting. He finished his meal as he had begun it, in silence, then rose and washed his dish and cutlery in the sink, put them to dry on the yellow rubber draining board and took up his stand in the middle of the kitchen floor. He stood with his feet spread apart, his hands by his side, looking down on her.

"Ma," he said, "I'm going to marry the tinker girl."

He had not been sure what sort of reaction he would arouse: a fainting fit, a burst of invective, a curse on his head, or even a blow. He watched the purple lips twitch, purse and twitch again. She didn't look up from her knitting and the gnarled arthritic fingers seemed to move even faster.

"Get your things and get out of this house and never cross that threshold again."

The words came from her in a steely cold tone he had never heard from her before. He stood momentarily non-plussed, immobilized in the middle of the kitchen floor. Several phrases came to his mind, but he found himself unsure of which to use and so said nothing. After half a minute of silence, in which he could hear the ticking of the clock, the click of the needles, and the soft suspiration of the turf burning in the stove, he turned and walked into his bedroom. He began to select the clothes he would take and other personal items, putting them in a battered suitcase and a pillowcase snatched from the bed. He stood trying to decide between one thing and another: a radio that worked on batteries, a polychrome statue of the Blessed Mother and another of St. Joseph, an oleograph of the Sacred Heart of Jesus on the wall, his fishing tackle, some magazines and a few books. He found it painful to elect one item over another, and again found his hands trembling. It was half an hour before he emerged, carrying the suitcase and the pillowcase stuffed with clothing, his cap on his head, the fishing tackle under his arm. He paused at the kitchen door to announce, "I'll have to make two trips."

He waited for her reply.

"Out!" she cried, waving her knitting at him, "out! And don't come back. There'll be no second trip."

He turned on his heels and left. He had not gone ten yards when he heard steps behind him and felt his right leg seized. For a split second he thought it was Zeke, his collie. It was his mother on her knees.

"Paddy! Paddy! Ye can't leave me. Come back."

He dropped his two bundles and raised her to her feet. "It's not just me, Ma. It's her too. I'm going to marry her."

Her face was only two inches from his face now and he could see it changing color. He threw his shoulders back to be farther from her, and saw with alarm her twisting lips and the hatred in her eyes.

"Yer an evil son to leave yer mother for a tinker whore."

"Don't say that, Ma. Don't say that."

"What would yer father say? A Madigan married to a tinker whore!"

He wanted to slap her face to stop her mouth, and to save himself from doing so he picked up the valise, and the stuffed pillowcase, and the fishing tackle. But he did not yet turn away from her.

"May God damn you and the devil take the two of ye. This is a mother's curse on an evil son."

He looked at her quietly for a short interval and then without a word turned and walked off. He felt a stone strike him and another land beside him in the road. Tears filled his eyes and ran down his cheeks but he was unable to brush them away. Behind him he could hear her cursing again but he could not make out the words she said.

He walked slowly with his awkward burden of luggage, stopping several times to hitch the fishing tackle under his arm, coming at last to the path that led to the neighboring Sullivan farm. He had to put all his gear down to open the iron gate between the stone posts that led to the house, shift it inside, and then close the gate behind him. When he arrived at the door of the house, it was already opened. Eithne Sullivan, whose black hair and white arms he had so often admired from afar, welcomed him.

"I saw you coming, Paddy. Welcome to you. Would you be going on a trip?"

He managed to stammer, "I've left home." She led him into the living room just as Michael Sullivan came in from an adjoining room, neatly dressed in clean brown work clothes, his bald head gleaming and his black hair combed slickly along the side. He was a big man, not much taller than Paddy but even huskier. He had overheard them.

"Is it left home, you have?"

Paddy nodded. "I was wondering if I could use your telephone to get a car here for me?"

Michael took him to the telephone and left him but had to return when the dial proved too new for Paddy to master. Michael dialed the presbytery and then put the phone in Paddy's hands. The curate answered.

"Could you come and drive me to Mrs. McCann's?" he asked softly. "I've left home."

"And where are you, Paddy?" came the brisk voice of the curate, Father Holland.

"At Michael Sullivan's."

"I'll be right along." Paddy was grateful for the quick response; he knew that Father Curtin had prepared his assistant to be ready.

He returned to sit with the Sullivans in their living room. He remembered it from before but it had not appeared as impressive as it did now with its armchairs, a large console radio, an upright piano and a picture window that looked out on the rolling line of the mountains. How did they do so well with a farm not much larger than his own? Eithne looked up from her crocheting and Michael from a Dublin newspaper. "Is everything all right?"

"It is," he said. "I thank you for that."

"Not at all. Not at all," said Michael. "Can I give you a mouthful of anything while you're waiting? A bit of the creature?"

"That would help indeed," he said. "The walk was short but the luggage was. . . long." He smiled faintly at his own pleasantry, and Eithne smiled back. Michael passed him a glass of whisky.

"I'll not join you if you don't mind, Paddy," he said. "I've only just finished a drink."

"Slainte!" Paddy said, holding the glass out toward them. He sipped slowly, not wanting to talk and glad to be occupied until Father Holland came. He knew that both his host and hostess would be eager to know why he had left. He somehow didn't dare say he was to be married, almost as if he didn't believe it himself and that a mention of it might banish it out of existence, like a wisp of bog cotton before the west wind. He was afraid as well that the mention of the tinker girl might raise in them a show of contempt.

"Will you stay in Sneem?" Mrs. Sullivan asked, looking up from her needlework.

"I will," he said. "I'm to work for Mr. Mulcahy and room with Moira McCann."

"That will be a change."

"It will."

"Your mother will miss you," she said.

Paddy rose suddenly. "I think that's him," he said. He was lying, but he wanted to get free of questions, overt or implied. He stood outside for several minutes before returning.

"Who is it that's coming for you?"

"Father Holland."

"Oh, Father Holland. Well, he knows the way, but Paddy, I would have taken you in town."

"Thank you. You would, I know; but it was arranged."

The wait seemed to him to be interminable. When the automobile came at last, they all went out to greet it. He wondered for a moment if his shyness had been only the fear of telling them he was to marry a tinker girl. He hated his own lack of courage. He wanted for a moment to go back and tell them, but the new life was underway. They would know soon enough; the whole town would know.

Father Holland, almost as young as Paddy and vibrant and vigorous, was an Irish speaker. He was annoyed to learn that Paddy knew no Irish.

"I'm afraid not. I left school very early."

"Weren't they teaching all the subjects in Irish?"

"Not one. It was a class by itself, and sure I never got on in it."

Father Holland shook his head in dismay. "And did your father know none?"

"He died when I was very young."

"And your mother?"

"She has no sympathy with it; none at all."

Father Holland, who was driving with his head bent over the wheel, now threw it back in annoyance. "I must start a class," he said, "for the men and women of your generation."

Paddy found that the interlude took his mind off the house and the woman he had left behind.

When Father Holland stopped at the home of Mrs. McCann, he sprang from the automobile and helped Paddy carry his luggage. Paddy thanked him and closed the door behind him, and hung his head. He felt a new surge of dismay. His mind ran back to a moment he had tried to ignore, but which had become a swollen embarrassment in his heart. He knew now that his reluctance to discuss his marriage with the Sullivans was a fear of telling them it was the tinker girl he was to marry, the one who had been beaten by her father, and who had run away, and had been found half-dead in the derelict boat. His shame rankled and he determined never again to hesitate. He would make his own world, their world, and be his own man.

"Am I truly twenty-two years old?" he asked himself aloud, "and a grown man?"

15

"I TOLD HER, FATHER."

"She was angry?

"She stormed, Father. She ordered me out of the house. She told me never to come back. She called me an evil son and cursed me. She said you were putting me up to it."

"Paddy," the priest said, "it's time for you to marry. You want a strong girl who trusts you and will work. I'm certainly going to help you. Mulcahy will hire you."

"My mother said it's not right for me to marry a tinker. That's she's a whore. She'll leave me and go back to the roads and what do I do then?"

"She's not a whore, Paddy, and if you don't want her she will go back to the roads. You don't wish that on her, do you?"

Paddy sat well forward in the large red leather chair near the hearth in the parlor of the presbytery, twisting his cap in his hands. He did not answer. He would feel strange away from the farm. He knew nothing else. The room at McCann's left him uneasy, there was such a neatness about it, and he missed the smell of burning turf. But he ached for intimacy, the dimensions of which his mind could not measure, certainly not in words.

"It isn't because she's not pretty?"

He dropped his head and studied the floor. His indecisiveness left him all but rocking from side to side. She wasn't pretty as Bessie Thompson was pretty and yet when he had seen her in Dr. O'Brien's office two weeks after he had found her, out of bed and on her feet, dressed in new clothes, she was transformed. Her hair had been washed and curled and the light green cotton dress, the color of the inside of a wave turning over, outlining her breasts, revealed a figure that he had not thought she had. Her nylon stockings and slingback shoes looked stylish. She had risen shyly from a chair in the office when he entered and stood speechless waiting for him to speak. Although he had kissed her when he was allowed for the first time to visit her bedside, and when she seemed so helpless, there was something about her now that intimidated him. She seemed so well-groomed, so self-assured.

"Hello, Jane," he said. "You're better."

She ran forward and embraced him and sobbed on his shoulder. The feel of her body in his arms and her breasts against him and the faint odor of lemon soap elated him. He found himself once again talking more than he ever did, unconscious of the presence of Dr. O'Brien, which, on another occasion, might have left him tongue-tied. He was recounting how he had felt when he searched for her and how he had staggered through the low tide water, slipping on the seaweed, along the shore until he got to the Bunnow pier, and how he knew she would be on one boat or another because when they had been fishing she had talked about boats carrying people to Paradise. He told her that he would have his own boat one day and they'd fish together three times a week in good weather or bad.

His mind came back to the priest's question. "It isn't." he said. "It isn't that she isn't pretty. Her smile is pretty. Her hair."

Father Curtin waited, but when he saw that nothing more was to be said he spoke again: "It's not that you are afraid of your mother surely since that's all over now. You've told her."

Paddy shook his head. "She may come after me. And the farm. . ."

"You are your own man now, Paddy," Father Curtin said. "You'll be working for Mulcahy and we'll get you and Jane quarters in the village here. And I'm sure if you ask him, Mulcahy will let you have the bicycle or we'll get you one. It's a new beginning, Paddy, and you'll be happy married. As to the farm, your mother can find hired hands ready enough."

Paddy dropped his cap and awkwardly picked it up.

"Now, Paddy," Father Curtin said in a sterner tone than he had used before, "you came to me suffering, saying you wanted to marry and you wanted to take out Bessie Thompson. She'll be married in a day or two herself and gone from the town. This you know. Jane's a very attractive young woman, Paddy, and about your age. Not that age is a factor. In any event put Bessie Thompson out of your mind."

Paddy nodded. He hoped by hanging his head that the priest would not notice how flushed his face had become. He couldn't bring himself to say what was true enough, that Bessie Thompson had long been out of his mind. He sat silent.

"And yet you are still undecided, even though you told your mother than you are going to marry Jane, even though you want to marry, and even though there is a young lady who will have you. Paddy, Paddy, she's a good looking woman, she's healthy and strong, and willing, eager." He paused. "She loves you."

"I. . . love her. . . I think. It's something else."

Father Curtin waited, his eyes fixed on the bent figure. Paddy could feel those eyes upon him. He fussed with his cap and looked at the hands of the priest with the fingertips pressed together. He felt himself half rise from the chair with a cry of anguish that came out of him despite himself.

"She told me about her father. . . about his. . ." He could go no further.

"About his raping her?"

Paddy fell back into the chair. "She told me," he said.

They had been walking together on the quay in a soft rain misting on the warm west wind. She was dressed as beautifully as Bessie Thompson, he said to himself, with a bright green shrug, hand-knitted, about her shoulders, over a figured cotton dress, her arms and legs bare, leather sandals on her feet. A black-headed gull swooped so close they had to duck and their heads touched, and he sensed a fragrance he knew to be cologne. They stopped by a massive bollard of stone and stood looking across the deck of a fishing dragger. He had not proposed to her as Dr. O'Brien had suggested, but talked simply as if it were understood that they would be married and find a room in the village and begin their life together. It was then, with the black-headed gulls drifting above them and six snowy swans on the far side of the inlet and a scarf of mist flung low over the water, that she told him. She did not look at him but kept her gaze fixed steadily above the dragger's cabin.

The shock made him forget the first words she used, blunt and plain, but he could hear the agony in her voice as she continued: "Not once, a dozen times." Then she collapsed in tears. "Oh, why did I ever tell you!"

He hated himself because he had made no answer, because he did not speak for minutes, even let go of her hand, and, more stupidly, blew his nose. How it must have hurt her to tell!

He was barely able to talk of it to the priest. Perhaps Father Curtin knew all along. She had hinted at that, although in his turbulence of mind he could not be sure. He feared the attitude the priest might take.

"That was noble of her," Father Curtin said. "Perhaps not wise—but noble. She must love you very much indeed, Paddy."

Noble? He had not expected that.

"I told her, Paddy, that she had no obligation to tell you. I told her that it was her secret. That the cruel life she knew was behind her and to be forgotten. I think the fact that she told you is a measure of how much she loves you and how much she trusts you, and how much she respects you. Trust, Paddy, is the measure of love, as we trust in God. We put our trust in Christ, and for love of Him, we must put our trust in one another."

Paddy felt too embarrassed to speak again, but he knew that he had to press on. "I thought she would be a virgin, Her own father—it's the worst sin."

"But not her sin, Paddy! Not her sin. Chastity is in the heart, mind and soul. What the flesh may do through coercion or fear, because of terror, or under torture does not have our consent. Actions are evil only when we consent."

The words came to Paddy as a blinding illumination. He felt as if he had been crawling through a tunnel of muck and suddenly saw, felt, understood, was caught up in a wave of flame. He did not understand it thoroughly, but he knew that the priest was telling him what he wanted to tell himself. She had made no excuse for herself. She never mentioned the beatings she had endured. She never cursed her father but it was obvious that she was terrified of him. His own unwordable fear of his mother should have made him immediately quick to understand what she had suffered. Her fear was the same sort of fear that had crippled him over the years and had left him what he was, half a man. They had parted without kissing, and he had walked home, half sickened, unable to go into any pub with his friends. He had sat in the McCann's barn unable to stomach the bread and cheese he had taken from the pantry, then he had wandered back to the pier where she had told him and his mind walked with her again on the other pier where they had fished together on what had been for him The First Day of the Existence of the World. The reverie made him miss the first words of Father Curtin's next remarks.

". . . from a life of terror and horror, Paddy. You must see that it is you who brought her out. Rescuing her from the rotting hulk when she was beaten and bleeding was praiseworthy, it took intelligence and the courage of persistence. But to rescue her from her sordid life with that hideous man, that will be heroism. You will show her that what was an act of disgust and horror for her can be the sweetest relationship the body can know. You are not afraid?"

He had expected the priest to say something quite different. He would not have been surprised at censure or even disdainful condemnation.

"Then you knew all along."

"I was the first one she ever told. But I couldn't tell you. It was her secret. She lived a life of squalor and pain—and Paddy, thank God for this, she never lost her inward nobility. These are things I understand, things I have dealt with in the confessional. She is a good woman, freed for the first time in her adult life from torment, with a chance for another life before her, sharing comforts she had never known, affection she had never known. And she risks throwing it all away because she would have no secret from the man she loves, nor would she withhold from him information about herself which could—if he chose—make him reject her."

Paddy felt his face flush again, and a knife blade cut across his heart. He rose quickly and awkwardly. "I've got to see her. I just didn't understand. The things we're told, you know. Things my mother said. . ."

He felt tears coming to his eyes and so he turned his head away as Father Curtin rose to face him.

"I've hurt her, Father, don't you see? That's the terrible thing, I've hurt her."

He ran from the presbytery toward the doctor's house, invigorated by the priest's words, and full of purpose, only to come to an anticlimax. Jane and the doctor had gone to Killarney and would not be back until the next day. He saw it as a punishment upon him that he must bear his remorse for twenty-four hours without her forgiveness, if she could forgive. No, he could not bear it for twenty-four hours. He would come in the morning first thing.

16

HE ARRIVED AT Dr. O'Brien's house early the next day. It was a mile from Mrs. McCann's but he got a lift the minute he ran down her clay path that was so brightly flanked by variegated flowers, blooming, budding, and the roses raising perfume on the air. The sedan that stopped for him was driven by an elderly man, vibrant and voluble who finally became enraged at Paddy's inability to follow the conversation or answer his questions. Paddy could think only of Jane and what he would say to her.

"What are you? Stupid?" the old man asked in irritation, running a hand over his balding head as he dropped Paddy off at the bridge.

"I'm very sorry," Paddy said in his haste. "I am that. Stupid."

"Wise guy!" the man snarled and spun his wheels to blister the rubber as he drove away.

Paddy ran to the rear door of Dr. O'Brien's house, a door that opened into the kitchen. In response to his knocking, Jane opened the door, a plastic apron over her print dress. She looked at him and smiled without speaking. He snatched the cap from his head and gestured with it.

"Please," he said, "come with me." He swallowed hard, upset that he was not more articulate or courtly. He watched her put her apron aside and admired the grace of her movements. He could not fathom why he was more intimidated by her now, dressed in the village clothes that Dr. O'Brien had bought for her, than he had been when she was wearing her wellingtons and her noisome plaid blanket. She seemed more a child then, not so much the mature woman. Certainly, the simple cotton dress she was wearing revealed the femininity of her body that the blanket had hidden and he was conscious that the affection he had had for her on that first day on the pier when they had fished together had deepened into passion and desire. He knew somehow that her maturity had bred a sense of maturity in him, a maturity that he had learned he lacked only when happily it had come to him.

He watched her go to the front of the house, evidently to tell Dr. O'Brien that she was going out. He was not put off that she came out without speaking to him, although he prayed that it was not because of resentment. She was so quiet by nature, so taciturn with him, that he thought with no certainty that she might be intimidated because of his few years of schooling.

Was she so quiet with the doctor? He led her along in silence, determined on a course of action thoroughly planned to redeem his earlier discourtesy. He held her left hand in his right hand and walked briskly. She offered no resistance but kept his pace. Two women, former friends of his mother, acquaintances of his, greeted him pleasantly, but he did no more than nod to them lest conversation draw from the fund of psychic strength he wanted for the ritual he planned.

They came at length to the same massive stone bollard on the edge of the pier against which they had leaned when she had shocked him with her confession. Now he stood facing her across it. He put his hands on it and stared at her.

"Jane," he said, as formally as he had ever spoken in his life, "I am twenty-two years old and you are nineteen. I have had some schooling. I can read and write and figure. But I'm not clever or wise. I have been laughed at in this town. There is an Irish word—omerdhan—that has been put on me more than once. Once I heard a man chide his son, 'Would you be wanting to grow up like Paddy Madigan now, would you?'" He felt her squeeze his hand in hers and he continued: "I know what he meant. I've never been off the farm in my life—and it isn't even mine."

He paused and took both her hands in his and kissed them on the backs and then on the palms. A young man in a suit and tie, dressed for an appointment, paused to stare at them, but hurried on. Paddy scarcely saw him, nor did he recognize the green dragger slowly nudging alongside the granite pier after a night's fishing.

"I hurt you the other day by being slow and stupid. Little of the world is with me. I mean to say. . ."

He could not finish the sentence because her lips were on his, and again taking her in his arms he found himself at the center of his magic circle of contentment which he had discovered on the First Day of the Existence of the World. Tears could come easily to him, but when he felt tears on his face he realized they were hers.

"Sorry to interrupt you, mate," a strong masculine voice called. "Can I throw you a line?"

Paddy fell back in alarm, blushed sheepishly, and looked down from the pier onto the deck of the dragger on the bow of which a young man stood with a hawser in his hands, a knitted blue hat on his head and a pleasant smile on his broad face. Having caught Paddy's attention, he flung the looped hawser through the air. Paddy caught it and slipped it over the glossy head of the bollard and looked at Jane and laughed. She was wiping her eyes with a handkerchief, and smiled. The line secured, Paddy turned to her.

"Do you forgive me?"

She nodded, and then nodded again. "I love you, Paddy," she said.

The young man had climbed onto the pier and was making a second line fast.

17

IT WAS THE DAY he was to work for Mulcahy.

"Now then, Paddy," said Mr. Mulcahy, "I'm going to tell you fairly. I will hire you to work for me five days a week, knowing that sooner or later you'll go running back to your ma and the farm because you'll have to. I'm hiring you because I have some land I want fenced and then cleared, and when it's fenced and cleared, I want it planted and tended. Fenced, cleared and planted. Now then, you may go back to your mother or you may not go back to your mother, but if you go back to your mother, I want your promise now that even then you will give me three days a week until the work is done.

"I shan't be going back."

"I hear you and I believe you but, Paddy, I've known your mother longer than you have. She has a wheedling way with her and you're a good boy and a soft boy and she'll be after you with promises if you go back, she and her wheedling way. And I'm not the one to say to you do or don't. I am only saying this as clearly as I can that you may go back and if you do go back I want your promise now that you will continue to give me three days a week." Mr. Mulcahy leaned against his small black truck and wiped his forehead with a large red bandanna. He swallowed, coughed and wheezed, leaving his face as red as the bandanna itself.

"I give you your promise," said Paddy. His head swam with happiness since Mulcahy was going to pay him six times what his mother had allowed him. The largess was such that it was with great difficulty that he brought himself to open the question of the bicycle. He swallowed several times before he decided on the boldest way.

"Can I use the bicycle to get back and forth?"

Mr. Mulcahy, restoring the bandanna to his hip pocket, looked at Paddy with some surprise. "Ye have none?"

"I do not," said Paddy lamely, and then thinking some explanation was required he began to tell the farmer that he had been saving up to buy one.

"Keep saving," his employer said. "Aye, keep saving. If you save, you'll have and if you do not you'll have naught. Use the bicycle by all means until you can afford your own. But get yourself a pair of clips, for without them you can catch your trousers on your laces and kill yourself in a tumble. Buy yourself a pair of clips."

"Thank you kindly," said Paddy nodding his head, "I'll get me clips." He paused and continued, "If you don't mind, I'd ride back on the bicycle now and be over first thing in the morning."

"Prompt is prompt and late is waste," said Mr. Mulcahy. "God speed ye." Paddy watched Mr. Mulcahy turn and puff back across the yard to the great house. He had had difficulty paying attention to the man's repetitious talk because his emotions were in turmoil. He could think only of Jane—Jane hurt, Jane suffering, Jane in tears, Jane kissing him and Jane nodding that she would marry him. The day for the wedding had been set but he could hardly bear to think of the change it would make in his life. He knew he felt more trepidation at facing the world away from his farm than Jane felt leaving the caravan and life on the roads.

18

THE PRESBYTERY WAS abustle when Paddy arrived too early but eager for the protection of its walls, anxious and fearful that his mother might find him and confront him. His fear of her was a fever that came and went. When its waves were on him, they drowned all concern with the tremendous alteration that had come over his life. Although he enjoyed the work at Mulcahy's and the companionship of the two men he worked with—something new to him after his isolation on his mother's farm—he had lost the sense of security that had been his when he lived at the farm. He felt exposed. The room at Mrs. McCann's, despite the maternal affection she wove him in, was a foreign country, a strange alien place where the eyes of Jesus of the Sacred Heart stared at him without benevolence and with rebuke. He went to sleep each night saying the rosary, asking God to reassure him he was doing the right thing. He had ridden to the presbytery on the bicycle as if he were breaking through a barrier of viscous air, but though he was nervous, he was firmly resolved. As he watched the preparations of the wedding in one room and the preparations for the breakfast in another, he was touched by a sense of elation easing his nervousness, or replacing it with a nervousness of a different sort.

Mary Condon, Father Curtin's housekeeper, venerable and English-born, although she had been in the town for more years than most of its inhabitants, seemed to take a new lease on life and planned and worked as if the queen of England, whom she—almost alone among the villagers—still esteemed, were to be the guest of honor.

"We haven't had a wedding in the rectory since before the troubles," she said to Father Holland, speaking as if Paddy weren't present. "Sure, they all want the high altar and a mass and a covey of bridesmaids these days. Isn't it like old times, although we never had the wedding breakfast here before. I suppose the poor lad has no home to speak of, nor she, a wanderer all her life." She glanced quickly over her shoulder for fear Paddy had heard her. He had, but he made no sign of recognition. She stood back and surveyed the table. "Och," she cried, "and that mother of his!" This time Paddy jumped at the mention of his mother and looked nervously toward the front door. Mrs.Condon shook her head and hurried out to the kitchen.

Relieved that his mother was not at the door, Paddy smiled to himself and wondered why he was not offended but amused by Mrs.Condon's remarks. There was a day he would have been; now he saw the housekeeper as another ally, and his mother in a new light. It all had something to do with his new beginning, although he did not quite understand it himself. With some assurance he arose and looked in a mirror over the fireplace with its turf fire smoldering. He settled his necktie and pushed back his black curly hair from his forehead and felt his chin to make sure he had shaved well, although there would be nothing he could do about it now.

At this moment Jane's image loomed in his mind, standing opposite him beside the bollard and moving her face forward to kiss him.

"Good morning to you, Paddy!" It was Father Curtin. Paddy turned and impulsively stepped forward and grasped the hand of the priest. It was the first time he had ever done so, but his feeling of gratitude overcame all sense of distance between them. Father Curtin seemed at once surprised and pleased. He shook Paddy's hand firmly with a strong grasp.

"Mary's putting her best foot forward," he said, laughing. "This is a big event for her. We haven't ever had a wedding breakfast here, but I'm rather in the role of father of the bride. It's most convenient to have the wedding here and the breakfast as well. Sit down, Paddy, we have a little time."

He turned and went off. Paddy knew that the wedding and breakfast were being held at the presbytery rather than the church and an inn to be safe from his mother's possible intrusion. He pictured himself and Jane at the altar of the church and his mother suddenly appearing from nowhere to cry out her denunciations and blaspheme before the very Body of Christ in the tabernacle. The fever of fear swept over him.

If she came to the rectory the curate could bar her or eject her if she came in and made a scene, with no one in town the wiser. He was fairly certain she would not come, probably had not heard that the wedding was to be held that day, but he knew that one day, once again, she would confront him and curse him and he shrank from the thought. He heard the doorbell ring, saw Father Holland hustle through the hall, and then, his heart shook and his palms grew wet as he saw Jane, a sturdy white wraith, partly concealed behind Dr. O'Brien, move toward the rear of the house. He ran his sweating palms on the outside of the trousers to dry them.

"Why is all this being done for me?" he asked himself, almost aloud. And then he remembered the day he had stopped Father Curtin outside the presbytery to say he wanted to marry—a twenty-two-year old man acting like a child.

"Who'd have him?" he had heard someone cry out with laughter in a pub one day, and he half feared it was himself that was being spoken of, only to learn it was an aging farmer in the next town whom Paddy envied and admired, a man he deemed more worthy than he. Again: "Who would have a tinker girl but another tinker?" he had heard said years before, and he thought of Jane.

"But they don't know her," he said this time aloud, startling himself out of his reverie, relieved that no one had heard him. The reflections had centered his thoughts on her and his whole being warmed, a different sort of fever.

"It's time, Paddy," the curate called, looking in the doorway. "Michael Sullivan's here."

His old neighbor was to be the best man and Dr. O'Brien the maid of honor. As Paddy rose to follow the curate, the front door bell rang again and his Uncle Francis, the widower of his mother's sister, arrived from Killarney. There was no time to do more than shake hands and all were ushered into the library. Jane stood beside Dr. O'Brien to the left of Father Curtin, who had donned an embroidered stole and held a missal in his hands. Paddy was unable to take his eyes off Jane, who, having looked at him with her face glowing , dropped her eyes.

Father Curtin called them each by name and then began, "You are about to enter on a solemn and holy pact, to share a sacrament instituted by Christ for the strengthening or your mutual love."

In his nervousness, Paddy heard no more that he could remember afterwards. The vision of his mother clutching his legs as he left home, the sound of her voice blistering him with vituperation came into his head at what he knew was the wrong moment, and yet he could not rid himself of the sight or the sound. He threw his shoulders back in an effort of concentration on the ceremony in time to answer the response in a firmer tone than he had ever used before, an exaggerated, "I do!" Her voice, soft as ever, was almost inaudible in the aftermath of his. Michael provided him with the ring. He slipped it over the finger that had held his father's ring which he had given to her when he found her battered and weak on the derelict dragger. She had had to wind it with adhesive tape to make it fit. And now the ceremony was ended. She kissed him and cried, and turned from him to embrace Father Curtin and then sob uncontrollably, but was soon calmed.

"It's happiness," Dr. O'Brien whispered in Paddy's ear. "She's not afraid anymore."

Mary, who had been drying her own tears in the doorway, led them into the larger room where the breakfast table had been set. Paddy became conscious that the others were waiting for him to lead the way. He had never before been such a center of attention. He looked hopefully at Jane who, taciturn as always, merely looked back at him. He felt someone take his arm, and having crooked it, place Jane's inside it. It was Dr. O'Brien, who now gave him a gentle nudge forward. He responded quickly, grateful for the help. Only Mary was ahead of them in the breakfast room, beckoning them to two chairs at the head of the table, a large window behind them and the sun streaming in. When Mary had seated them, Paddy looked at the others. On his right was

Father Curtin, Dr. O'Brien and his Uncle Francis, a tall man, grizzled and wizened like his sister-in-law long alienated from him. On Paddy's left beyond Jane was Father Holland, Mary and Michael Sullivan, whose Eithne was ailing and could not attend. Paddy suddenly became aware of his social duties.

"Uncle Francis," he said, "you are most welcome. I could no more than shake your hand when you came in. It was the last minute."

"Thank you, Paddy," the man said without rising. "I'm proud to be here; I never thought I'd live to see the day, Paddy. I thought it would never come."

Even when he was seated Francis appeared tall and his bass voice was loud. His white hair was thick and full on top of an extremely narrow face, the features of which had always reminded Paddy of a hawk. He had not seen the man in years but his childhood impression was justified. Michael Sullivan arose, his bald pate shining.

"You make a grand couple," he said, "and here's a toast to the two of you: Slainte! Slainte! Slainte! for many, many years and may all your children be twins and no year without a pair."

Paddy took up the footed glass before him and with the others joined the toast and then felt perhaps he should not have. It was the first time he had tasted champagne. He thought he would have preferred a glass of stout.

"Am I supposed to say anything?" he whispered to Father Curtin.

"Not unless you wish to."

"I do." In spite of his embarrassment he rose to his feet and faced the group.

"Paddy has a word." The clerical voice cut through the conversations. All eyes turned toward him, and for a long moment he regretted his boldness. At last his sense of elation overcame his shyness and he said, "I am grateful to you all. Indeed, it's grateful I am. To all of you, very grateful."

He began to fill up and sat down quickly, shaking. He reached down to pick up the napkin he had dropped and felt Jane's hand on his left arm, a reassuring grasp. Please God, it will be there always. The talk ran among the other men. Mary was up and down, bringing in dishes, serving them all, and managing occasionally to eat a bite herself.

"I should be helping," Jane whispered to Paddy in a moment when the others seemed not to be noticing them.

Paddy replied, "I don't think so." But Jane arose and went to Mary's side just as she was clearing away some salad dishes. Paddy watched anxiously, afraid of some breach of manners.

"Sit down, child," said Mary, smiling and shaking her off-white hair. "This is your day. You'll he waiting on himself and others long enough."

Father Holland leaned over to Jane when she returned to her chair. "She'd rather do everything herself," he said. "It's her way."

The doctor told them they were to have her house all to themselves for the next three days while she went to Dublin,

"A medical convention," she said. "Jane knows where everything is, and what's to be done. She's had the run of the place before. I'm off right now, this minute."

Her departure signalled the end of the breakfast. Paddy rose to bid his uncle good-bye and noticed that Francis was talking more loudly than ever.

"I'll tell you why I came in at the last minute," he said in his deep voice. "I waited to make sure that old bitch wasn't here. She murdered her husband—nagged him to death, nagged him to death. He was a brother to me; and her own sister died of shame. That's why I waited until the last minute."

Paddy flushed as red as the fuschia hanging beside him and was afraid to look behind at the two priests.

"She wouldn't come," was all he could say.

"And God knows what she did with all the money. She wouldn't even buy him the medicines he needed. Bad cess to her. Don't remember me to her," the uncle cried. "Bad cess to her and the likes of her."

He bent down and kissed Jane, who received the somewhat alcoholic greeting stoically and bade the man farewell in a whisper.

"The Mulcahys couldn't come," Father Curtin said as he saw them to the door, "but Mr. Mulcahy asked me to give you this envelope."

Before Paddy could speak in reply, Mary came forward and kissed him and hugged him and then kissed Jane. Paddy made his thank-yous to them all and went into the street with Jane, unconscious of the eyes turned on them in their modest finery as he walked his bicycle toward the doctor's house with Jane beside him. He knew he was in a daze because the village looked as new to him as the necktie he wore. He thought he had never seen it before. He felt stronger than he had every felt in his life. He felt renewed.

"Come on, Jane," he said. "We'll have a glass of stout and toast ourselves."

"Mr. and Mrs. Madigan," she said. "Mr. and Mrs. Madigan."

19

AS PROMISED BY Dr. O'Brien they had her house to themselves.

"Let me make you some tea," she said to him as they walked into the kitchen and she turned to fill the kettle, put it on the stove and lighted the gas. He thrilled in their isolation, in her movements, in the cut of her wedding dress, and was admiring her when she same to him and sat in his lap. He closed his arms around her and crushed her in his happiness.

"We'll have the tea," she said, "and then I'll pour you a glass of stout." He pictured himself beside her in bed and wondered at his own patience.

As he drank the tea, she talked of the breakfast and revealed to him how embarrassed she had been with it all.

"It was much too grand," she said. "Didn't you find it much too grand?"

He nodded, and then he listened to her recount how she had first spoken to Father Curtin—"and him after catching me stealing from the church."

"Oh, God, you poor thing," said Paddy, "to be so wretched."

He knelt beside her chair and brought her head down to kiss it and they remained that way for minutes until the kettle whistled and she rose to refill the pot.

"Before we go to bed," said Paddy, "I want to walk you to the pier and kiss you there again."

She put the teapot back on the table, and ran her hand through his tumble of black curls, her blue eye and her dead eye facing him.

"You're a handsome man," she said, and laughed.

She changed her dress for the walk and as they went out of the house and through the square, Paddy was conscious of two dozen eyes upon them. "They know already that we're man and wife," he said. "And my mother knows, I'm sure." Jane did not speak and indeed was silent until they stood again at the massive stone bollard watching two men cleaning the decks of a green and rusted dragger.

They were alone, except for an old man in a tattered jacket who was painting an old black curragh that lay upside down at the end of the pier. Paddy looked for a moment at the tiny harbor, its boats and gulls and busy fishermen, and was about to call Jane, "Mrs. Madigan." But he realized he could not, because the name raised in his mind the picture of his mother, and brought again the sense of ingrown uneasiness. The concern was out of his mind when, returning hand in hand, they reached the house. He was anxious to make love to her and nervous about beginning, so that when she suggested that she prepare some dinner, he agreed, and helped her clumsily about the kitchen. It was early when they retired. Another strange room, he thought, on entering the room and examining the tiled bathroom off of it. His mind ran back to his old room at the farm and the lonesome, unhappy nights he had spent in it, and he thought of the room he had at Mrs. McCann's that seemed in retrospect so sterile.

Soon he must find quarters for the two of them, perhaps even in Castle Cove, which would be near Mulcahy's farm.

While Jane went into the bathroom to change, Paddy opened his suitcase and removed the long white linen nightgown that he usually wore. He preferred it to the flannel. He had never owned pajamas. He took off his shoes and placed them at the foot of the double bed with its glistening brass, and put his socks inside them. He hung his shirt and tie over the back of the chair, and waited for her to emerge. She came out in a diaphanous nightgown—given her, he guessed, by Dr. O'Brien—that revealed shimmeringly and alluringly her full figure.

"By God," he said, "you're lovely." And he hugged and kissed her before going into the bathroom. There he marveled at the modernity of the fixtures and set them for his shower. It was only the second time in his life he had had a shower. At home he had tubbed in the kitchen. It was a movable tub and had suited him fine, although he preferred the ocean. He almost scalded himself before he managed to readjust the stream of water from the glistening nozzle, and then luxuriated in the water and then in a warm turkish towel that had taken its heat from the proximity of the towel closet to the hot water heater. He emerged refreshed and invigorated, free of the sweat of nervousness that had doused him during the day. He found her lying in bed, smiling at him. With a sense of embarrassment, he walked past the foot of the bed to enter it from the other side, stepped inadvertently on his shoes, lost his balance, threw his arms up in the air to right himself and stumbled two steps to the side.

"Squawk! Squawk! Honk!" she cried out, and be blushed with shame at his awkwardness until he realized what had brought the sound from her. In the white nightgown, waving his arms in the air to catch his balance, he had made her, he knew, recall the great gray heron that they had startled at the pier their first day together, and the day he thought of as the First Day of the Existence of the World. She was laughing aloud now and her laughter banished his shyness. He grasped the brass rail at the foot of the bed, threw back his own head in laughter and shouted, "the heron!" She was still laughing when he vaulted over the rail at the foot of the bed, and lay beside her. When he approached he was conscious of a rigor of hidden terror in her and of his own timidity, but at length they found themselves in the depth of intimacy his virginity had not imagined, and what came over him was a preternatural release of personality.

After their love-making, she clung to him with a fierce strength which slowly relaxed only after minutes, and she became talkative in a way he had not heard before. Her taciturnity was banished for the moment, banished utterly, and she talked, not hysterically, but in a soft dreamy tone that he wished would go on forever, so that he was disinclined to interrupt her with his questions, or even with a kiss.

"I never knew the true tinker life," she said, "but a short time. We all were very close, the women and the children most of all. The men too. They drank a lot together. My Da too. The day Mammy died he fought. We always dig the graves for our own dead. It's the way.

"And Da fought with the men who helped him dig Mammy's grave. I don't know why. The week before they seen him punching up my mother. The only time I ever saw him do it. They didn't quarrel much. Nowhere near as much as the others. But he fought with the men, and they had just helped him dig her grave. When they buried her his right eye was black and swollen and shut. He nearly killed one of the men. He's very strong, my Da.

"I never seemed to please him after Mammy died. Maybe for a short while. But he broke my eye, that's why it's the way it is, and he broke my nose. Sometimes they say there's a curse on the tinkers so we always must wander, and I told the priest that when he said it was best I marry you. He laughed at it; but it may be there. I told him I might not be ready to be inside a house. I've never known it." She fell silent.

"How do you like this house?" He kissed her cheek.

"It's a grand house, to be sure, but I shouldn't be here, doing naught but sitting and eating."

"And getting well."

"Oh, I'm fine now. But I would be doing something."

"You can take care of me."

"I think I'll like that fine."

"We'll find our own quarters," he said.

"Will you miss the farm?"

He couldn't answer, but she resumed. "My Da helped me for a while, but he wouldn't let me be in school. Ah, I would be heart-scalded when children littler than me could read and my good eye no good to be there at all. I know a song or two by heart and I made up some of my own, and I know a prayer."

"Say the prayer," he said.

"I'd be nervous."

"Never with me," he said. "Never be nervous with me."

She paused and took his hand in hers. "Hail, Mary, full of grace, the Lord is with thee. Blessed art thou amongst women."

Again she was silent.

"Go on," he said.

"That's all."

"Oh, there's more to it than that," he said. "I'll teach it to you."

"Teach me to read," she said.

"I will. I will indeed, and to count and to add and subtract."

"I thought at first the prayer was about my mother because her name was Mary."

"Who set you straight?"

"Another tinker girl, who had been to the nuns and she told me about Christ and his mother, the Blessed Virgin, and how he died. I cried when I heard it."

"And did your father tell you nothing about God?"

"He did a bit after that. Then I told him what the girl had said. But he hated the churches; he'd only go into the churches to steal. He made me afraid of priests and afraid of schools. I asked him to teach me the good things they taught in the schools. He told me a lot but then came the heavy boozing, he called it."

"I'll get books and I'll read them to you."

"I'd like that. And will we always be together?"

"Forever and ever."

"I forgot to tell you," she said as she dozed off. "I know about the Pope. I had a picture of him in the caravan."

20

"YER A DEVIL," she said. "A devil from hell. Turning my own boy against me."

Father Curtin looked down patiently at Mrs. Madigan.

"My understanding is that you turned him out of your house." He watched the twisting lips, the green eyes that alternatingly glared and shifted alarmingly from side to side. She wore her gray dress buttoned to the throat and over it a brown cardigan sweater. Her yellowy gray hair, badly soiled, was neatly braided, tightly pinned on her head, and drawn back so that her ears showed. She wore no hat. Her wrinkled face was sweaty from her exertion in walking into town, and dusty from the roads. He thought it was a strange contrast, the unwashed face beneath the dust, and the carefully braided hair. The eyes frightened him a bit, shifting as they did so wildly. There was a desperation in the woman that he sensed would stop at nothing.

"Sure, I'm trying to save him from throwing his life away on a tinker whore."

"I assure you the girl is not a whore."

"They're all whores. Don't be after telling me. Don't I know my own son and how he can be gotten around by a smooth word? He's a child. He's not right in the head. Wasn't he unable to finish school?"

"I was told you took him out."

"All lies! Who knows best for a boy? He's a fool like his father was before him, squandering money on books and the drink, and the likes of you preyed on him as well, with a rosary here and a rosary there. Ach. I'll have the law on ye this day before the sun sets."

She stood teetering in rage in the hallway of the presbytery. The pitch of her voice rose to such wrath that Mrs. Condon came out of the kitchen in alarm and stood in the far end of the hall. Mrs. Madigan glared and pointed at her.

"Another whore," she yelled. "The devil's whore."

Turning on her heel, she ran out the still open door. With short energetic steps she trotted to the office of Sergeant Callaghan, bursting in through the door and ignoring a woman in a flowered dress and pink turban who was reporting the theft of a bicycle.

"Arrest that priest!" Mrs. Madigan shouted. "He's corrupted my son. He's stolen my son away."

The woman at the desk pulled aside so quickly that she seemed to jump.

Sergeant Callaghan rose from his chair behind his desk and leaned forward across it. "Calm down, woman," he said. "Can't you see this woman is before you?"

"Bedamned to her," cried Mrs. Madigan. "I want my son back."

"Then why don't you speak to him? If it's Paddy you mean, he's reached the age of discretion."

"He has not. He's a stupid, evil child who has been betrayed."

The sergeant stepped from behind his desk. "Madam, your case is not with me."

Taking her firmly by the arm, he walked her to the door and thrust her out. She turned a purple face on him with quivering lips. "Yer all the same. Yer in league with hell."

She ran back to the road and along it for about fifty yards before pausing to signal an oncoming automobile to stop. It roared past her. Only strangers stopped to offer her a ride. Those who knew her ignored her signals, unless it was in a winter rain when conscience bade them stop and endure the serrations of her tongue.

A full week passed before she put on her Sunday best, flowered hat and all, and started for Mulcahy's new land far up the hill which was being fenced and cleared, where Paddy worked with an axe cutting and driving posts of holly and yew to string barbed wire. Two other laborers worked with him, in shirt sleeves with braces holding their trousers, grimy caps on their heads, one indistinguishable from the other. Paddy saw her coming long before she was able to distinguish him, and he dreaded the confrontation. He could feel his stomach tighten and his hands tremble. Rather than have his fellow laborers overhear what was sure to come, he dropped the axe and ran forward to meet her. As he went down the hill, he relived all his past anguish. In her haste, she stepped into a ditch and came out with her Sunday shoes and her woolen stockings covered with black muck above her ankles.

"What brings you to me, Ma?"

"Paddy," she said in a soft voice that he thought he had once heard far off but didn't recognize, "I can't go on without ye. I need ye on the farm. Come home to me, Paddy."

"I cannot," he said.

"Ah, ye can, Paddy," she said. "I'm sorry for all I said and did. Bring the colleen with ye. She'll be welcome."

He took off his cap and slapped it against his knee, more to give him time to think than to dismiss a bee.

"It's 'colleen' now, is it, and 'whore' no longer?" His voice quaked.

"It's only my way of talking. I couldn't bear to lose ye and I can't bear to have ye away now. Sure, ye know I can't carry on the farm alone or pay a hand. She'll be welcome indeed. Come back, Paddy. I'll give up the big room and the double bed and take your room and the three of us will live homely together."

He looked off into the distance where the river shone in shafts of sunlight through the broken clouds, and then down on the roof of the farmhouse that had been his only home.

"I'll have to talk to Jane," he said. "It will be for her to say, it's hers to decide. You put some hard words on her and there's an apology needed there."

"She'll have it, I swear."

"But even then she may not want to go."

"Paddy, tell her I've money—money and it will be yours one day. Money, ye see, that will help draw her."

"Go home, Ma," he said, "and I'll talk to her tonight. But I'm giving no promise."

"Yer a good boy, Paddy, I know. You were always a good boy, and yer my only child."

He watched her shrinking figure as she walked back over the half-cleared land and the black ditches like wounds in the soil, all lined with silver slivers of water, golden where the sun struck.

21

"I THINK YOU have to give her a chance," Father Curtin said. "But remember, Paddy, your first duty is to Jane. She must agree and with a full heart."

He repeated to Jane what his mother had said to him and what the priest had said. She looked at him steadily for a long while without speaking. He was taller than she and she had to strain her neck to look him in the eyes. She could see the agony moving like a shadow across his face, the question in his eyes, the quiver in his mouth. Ever since their first night together, ever since the day they had fished together at the stone pier, she knew that she would never say a word or take a step that would hurt him. The thought of going with him to the farm brought a cruel and vivid image to her mind: the contorted face of that bitter woman, the cane flashing in the air and striking her twice on the forehead before he could wrest it from her; her fright and flight and her head throbbing so as to dement her, until she collapsed.

"I'm so afraid of her, Paddy," she said. "It's so. It's afraid I am."

He took her in his arms and could feel the fear running through her; not that she trembled but that the muscles in her body seemed harder as she pressed against him and as he crushed her gently in his arms.

"Don't cry," he said. "I will not let her hurt you by her speech or any other way. She wants to apologize to you."

She had not been so happy in her life as in their two weeks together, an extended happiness that she had not believed possible. Her life on the roads had taught her that happiness of its nature did not last. Happiness was something snatched in the course of a cruel day, that came with a kind word from someone, or the gift of a large coin, a warmth in all the senses as one rode along in the sun in the caravan, or a dreamy moment by the fire at night or in the late twilight with the heat of the day still in the ground. It came walking with the dog, of bathing in the cool water of a lake, or fishing, or watching boats sail by. But it did not last, for it simply appeared in the interstices between blows and abuse and hunger and the terrible loneliness she had known and the evil she had endured. So this now must end.

The hospitality of Dr. O'Brien had been stretched beyond reason, and they had had no luck in finding other quarters in the town.

"Paddy, if you must, I'll do whatever you say."

"Father Curtin said we should give her her chance."

And so it was that they went to the farm, both riding on the Mulcahy bicycle, she on the handle bars and their wordly goods on the carrier rack.

"I have a surprise for you," he said.

"Have you now?"

"Your plaid blanket. I washed it before we knew you were lost. I thought I'd have it for you when we came together, but I had left it at the farm."

She laughed in delight but said nothing for a while.

"Do I want it, I wonder?"

"You'll never have to beg in it again," he said. "I'll see to that."

"It wasn't so hard, begging," she said. "I'd do it for you."

"Oh, God, no," he said. "It isn't right. Sure, I'd only feel half a man if I let you be doing that."

"I'd steal for you," she said, and she tried to turn and look at him so that he would see she was laughing.

"Stop codding me," he said.

"My father used to beat me if I didn't steal."

"I think I'd beat you if you did."

"Do you know that some tinker women are proud that their men beat them?"

"I don't believe that."

"Well, it's so."

They had come to the boreen and they dismounted and walked beside the bicycle as they went up to the door.

"Say that little prayer," he said.

She looked about the yard at the chickens and piled turf and under the metal canopy at the stored hay. Beside it stood an ancient stone shed where the cows took refuge in the worst weather. The dog danced out to greet them, and behind him briskly came Mrs. Madigan.

"You'll not be sorry ye've come," she said, "Ye're welcome indeed."

Paddy had never seen his mother dressed so proudly. Her hair had been washed and set, and he was sure there was rouge on the wrinkled cheeks. The green eyes still moved in their furtive shiftings, but her brown teeth showed in a smile and the lips so often pursed in irritation and anxiety were drawn back pleasantly. Her conscious effort at warmth set Paddy wondering as much as it reassured him.

"Girl," she said to Jane, taking her hands in hers, "I'm heartfelt sorry for the blows I struck. You are welcome here."

She led them into the kitchen and then into the room that had been hers.

"Here ye are," she said. "Ye'll find this home. I've cleaned out this bureau for yer things. Put them in there. That's a fine dress you're wearing."

"Thank you, ma'am. Dr. O'Brien gave it to me," said Jane.

"I've the kettle on and we'll soon have tea and some hot scones."

Two hours passed for Paddy in an air of unreality, an atmosphere he had never known in his maturity, but remembered faintly from childhood when his father had been alive and when, as a small child, he had seen guests come to the house and dine at their table.

22

THEY SAT THROUGH the evening listening to the radio. Paddy noticed that Jane, who was naturally taciturn, was even quieter than usual, quieter than she had been at mass when he endured the stares of congregants as he walked with her down the middle aisle and sat on the right hand side of the church beside her. Father Curtin had prepared her for Communion. She had told him that she had received Communion way back when her mother was still alive, but had no memory of being instructed. Father Curtin spoke to her about the sanctity of the sacrament, and she received beside Paddy with great reverence. She seemed oblivious to the eyes of the parishioners,who, now in full possession of the facts surrounding the romance and the wedding, were full of talk and interest about the tinker girl. A few stared, but the majority merely stole an occasional covert glance at her. Paddy wished he could remain as oblivious of them as she seemed to be.

Now she sat in the kitchen of the farmhouse with no words at all, far from oblivious to his mother's nervous presence. Paddy shared her discomfort. She listened intently to him when he spoke, and to his mother when she spoke, and to them both as they discussed what had happened on the farm in his absence and what needed to be done first of all, and how to arrange his schedule best so that he could fulfill his obligation to Mr. Mulcahy and work there three days a week. Then they all listened to the radio and a dramatic presentation that Jane told him later she didn't understand at all.

After it, he said to his mother, "Jane wants chores given her. Chores that will be her own. The cows? Sure, now, that might be just the thing."

"Would ye be liking that, girl?" Mrs. Madigan asked. It was only the second question the woman had put directly to her daughter-in-law that day. "I would," she answered softly, and looking up at Paddy, "I know the cows."

They retired early. Just before bedtime, Paddy and Jane walked along the boreen, past the fenced pasture, almost to the shore. The sky was filled with stars and the soft warm west wind moved about them like a living thing.

"We'll work together tomorrow," he said. "It's not until Thursday that I must go to Mulcahy's."

She made no reply. He was reassuring her. He stopped in the road and took her in his arms. She was wearing the plaid blanket he had washed, the old stench gone from it. He was conscious of the faint smell of soap from her throat, and his mind ran back to the bathroom at the doctor's house where, she told him, laughing at the recall, she had been schooled in a new state of cleanliness.

"I was such an innocent," she said.

"Do you miss the luxury of it?" he asked. "You're not afraid here?"

"I'm uneasy in the house," she said.

"Uneasy," he said resuming their walk. "Uneasy. I know that will pass. Do pray that it will work out."

He turned and kissed her, running his hand through the thick mass of her red hair.

"I know that prayer now," she said.

"Didn't Father Curtin teach you any others?"

"He told me to love God and His Son Jesus with my heart and my mind and that I could learn the prayers later." She took his arm in hers.

The next day they worked side by side, returning to the house for lunch and again for dinner. Mrs. Madigan put the evening stew out on the tan table before them, and then, without speaking, took up sewing by the stove. Paddy noticed that the smile had gone and the lips were pursed again, but when she finally spoke the words were pleasant enough.

In the late evening Paddy spent time teaching Jane to count and to add and subtract. She was as excited as a child and her blue eye glowed.

In bed that night, tired from their exertions of the day, they talked of its events. Jane was full of questions about the farm, which he answered sleepily.

"Can I go with you to Mulcahy's?"

He was dozing now. "I think," he said, paused and continued, "you should stay. . ."

"I'll bring you your lunch," she said.

He slept.

23

SOMEWHERE IN THE DISTANCE a dog barked and she heard Zeke give an answering growl. How strange it had all become: leaving off the old life, and taking on the new. The kindness of Father Curtin and Dr. O'Brien was a mystery to her. Yet she had seen something like it among some of the tinker women and children, a sense of family it was with some of them, such as she had been denied. She could see her mother somewhere above her and smiling at her; she remembered above all that smile.

Her father's image rose on her inward sight and she moved involuntarily, shrinking before it. More than ever she feared even the thought of him, his brutality and his lust which she dared not name to herself and which even before she understood it had sickened and frightened her. She drove his image from her mind by visualizing sums in addition and subtraction. Arithmetic had come to her quickly, more quickly than reading, perhaps because of her years of fingering the coins and not quite grasping their numerical relation. She recited the additional problems Paddy had given her at the table and was trying to add seventy-three and eighty-five in her mind when she dozed off.

In a while she woke again. She lay staring upward, warm from the bedclothes and the flannel nightgown he had bought her and warm from his presence. In the shadows she could barely make out the lines of his face, the tousled mop of curly hair, and the curve of his shoulder, not unlike the line of the nearest mountain. She linked her arm through his arm and tried to sleep, but something drove her to listen to Mrs. Madigan still moving about the kitchen, moving nervously it seemed. Somewhere inside the woman was something Jane feared. She remembered a stoat she had seen trapped in a cage, fretting to get out, making furious short dashes toward one wire side, biting the wires and backing off, turning to another side, and biting the wires there. As she dozed the sounds from the kitchen became the stoat's teeth on the wires, and just before she slept, the stoat was in the kitchen and Mrs. Madigan was off somewhere in a cage. Then it seemed the stoat was inside the woman, but she slept at last and did not dream.

In the morning, she rose early and milked the cows. With him she helped raise the giant aluminum cans of milk onto the donkey cart, and together they walked the team to the main road and the collection platform. He had put the bicycle on the cart, and brought it down and mounted it at the collection station. He kissed her goodbye and rode off to Mulcahy's. With the donkey bridle in her hand she watched him pedal along and felt a surge of pride she hadn't known since childhood, when she had been given at once a new pair of wellingtons and her first great shawl. The lovely sense of possession had sent her marching through the tinker encampment, in and out among the four caravans that were lined beside a great highway outside Galway. She recalled the happy day in all its wash of sunlight, a wall of purple fuschia, the odor of the campfire, the tinker women calling out to her in admiration and the grand smile on her mother's face as she returned to their caravan and bent her knees in what she took to be a curtsy, the first she had ever tried before an audience. Her mother's smile had grown into gay laughter and she had called to Mike to come out and see his colleen grown up. She had never had that sense of euphoria from that day to this vivid moment when she watched his broad back on the bicycle setting off for work. She turned the cart about and started back.

When she unhitched the donkey and put him in the pasture, she went into the house. She found the door of Mrs. Madigan's room, which had been Paddy's, closed and she could hear the woman moving about. She thought at first she was overhearing a conversation but then realized that the woman was talking to herself in curiously strident tones. Her sense of uneasiness returned and she went into the big bedroom where they had slept and started to make up the bed. Mrs. Madigan's talking to herself made her think again of the trapped stoat. She turned and looked out of the bedroom window at the lush green countryside, holding back the torn lace curtain with one hand, trying to shake the uneasiness. She shrugged her shoulders and resumed her work.

When at last she entered the kitchen with a pillowcase filled with soiled clothes, she found Mrs. Madigan preparing to make bread. "I had a mind to wash these clothes," she said, standing near the doorway.

"Put them in the hamper there. I'll do them all at once."

Jane did as she was told and then walked to the open door to stand in the sun, which had risen well above the undulating line of the mountains. She rubbed her bad eye as she gazed across the intersecting blues and grays and browns of the mountains, two of the crests still crowned with early morning mists.

Something in her yearned to be walking among the mountains through Ballybeam Pass and down the far-reaching slopes to Killarney and the lakes, and to stand at the brink of Ladies View and gaze over the silver waters. She loved Killarney. She felt at home in the cities and she wondered where her father might be. She had been told about the theft from Casey's home and of another farm that had been entered and ransacked but nothing taken, as if the thief were looking only for money or liquor. Stolen goods could be traced. She knew her father had sold stolen goods by the side of the road, but he had been careful whom he let buy and careful not to tell other tinkers of his depredation. ("Ye want someone who knows what he's getting and isn't going to ask questions.") She had been uneasy about that sort of thing, a different uneasiness than what assailed her now.

Paddy had encouraged her to pray as her father had not, and she did frequently now particularly in the garden and the fields. Having worked for a while in the garden, she went back to the kitchen. Mrs. Madigan was kneading dough on the side table, her sleeves rolled up above the elbows, baring her thin white muscular arms.

"May I make myself a cup of tea, ma'am?"

"Ye may."

Without a further word, Jane brought the kettle to the front of the stove to bring the simmering water to a boil, took some scones and bread from the colored tin, and, then, entering the cold closet brought out butter and marmalade.

She was conscious that Mrs. Madigan would glance over her shoulder at her every so often but no word was spoken.

"Would you be joining me for a cuppa?"

"Not now, girl; I'm too busy."

Jane brewed and drank her tea and finished her scones and marmalade, and began to prepare some sandwiches for Paddy. Mrs. Madigan put the brown dough in a large brown bowl. "What's that yer doing?"

"I told Paddy I'd bring him his lunch." As she looked up with her answer, she saw Mrs. Madigan striding toward her, her face plum-colored, her lips twisting and pursing in rage.

"I'll do that," she cried, her head wagging from side to side. "I'll do that!" She snatched bread from Jane's hands, took up a large knife ignoring the one in Jane's hand, and began to butter the bread with trembling hands. She was so positioned beside the table that Jane could not rise from her chair, and she was forced to sit watching the frenetic preparations.

Something inside Jane began to tremble, as if in rhythm with the woman's hands and the flash of the knife. The sort of fear she had had at night in the caravan, when she thought he might be approaching her, came over her, and yet she couldn't move from where she was. She understood dimly that something not wholly maternal but terrifyingly sexual was driving the woman, but she had no name to put on it. The knife in the woman's hand was better suited for carving stew beef than for buttering bread, and it moved so shakily as the woman plied it, that Jane felt fear turn to alarm.

As soon as she could do so without pushing the other aside, she slipped from her chair and stood nearby. Mrs. Madigan stuffed the sandwiches into a plastic bag, poured some milk into a jar, fastened the cap, and put it in the bag along with a thermos of tea that Jane had prepared. Then she turned and with a sudden movement thrust the bag into Jane's hands.

"Ye've a long walk. Don't dawdle. He's murdering himself up there in the field. Mulcahy the Thief."

"I'll hurry, ma'am," Jane replied and fled from the house. When she was fifty yards away she looked back and, not seeing Mrs. Madigan in the doorway, she paused to catch her breath and to see if she could quiet the palpitations in her breast. After a minute, she drew several deep breaths of the warm noon air, and started briskly along the boreen. Some rain came as she reached the main road but it soon went and the sun and the wind dried her cardigan and her hair. The turbulence of emotion had subsided, and the nearer she go to Mulcahy's the more it altered to a sense of pleasant expectation, and then to joy when she saw him piling stumps and logs not too far from the road. When he turned and saw her and waved, she laughed and ran forward happily. They sat together on one of the split stumps and shared the lunch.

"I'll not eat with you sitting there and not having a blessed morsel yourself."

"I'll take one of the scones," she said. "You'd better eat; you're all sweaty. Your shirt is soaking."

"Ah, sure, it's pleasantly warm and warmer still with you beside me. How did it go with herself down there?"

She decided not to tell him about the preparation of the lunch. "Can't I stay and watch you?"

"Sure I'd get no work done at all. I'd be looking at you forever."

She smiled at him and held his free hand in both of hers, so much whiter than his own. "How strong your fingers are!" she said, and she kissed his father's ring which she had put back on his hand after their wedding. She was reluctant to leave him and more reluctant to return to the farmhouse without him.

"I'll tell you what," he said. "Take these pound notes and walk toward Castle Cove. There's a little shop on the way: Mrs. Twomey's. On the left hand side of the road, you'll never miss it. Buy some cheese and some pound cake and what all and we'll have a party tonight. If you walk slowly, and enjoy the birds and the flowers, you'll find me through work when you get back and we'll go home together. I'll ride you home."

He kissed her on the forehead and turned and went back to where he had been piling stumps and logs. His fellow workers were already busy with their axes. She watched him for a moment, the strong surge of his muscularity as he picked up twisted logs and threw them on a growing pile. Then she turned for the road. The euphoria of pride of possession came back to her. She was happy to have him, happy to be cared for.

Her errand done at great leisure, they went home together on the bicycle, and walked together up the boreen with the machine between them, hands locked together on the handlebars.

Mrs. Madigan was in the doorway in her gray dress and tattered jumper. Seeing them approaching, hands joined, she called out. "Where has she been all afternoon that she comes home with you now?" Jane noticed that the whine had returned to the voice and she saw the head wagging with the words.

"She was buying you a bit of brack and some chesse and a trifle. We thought we might have a party like."

As Jane came closer she could see the green eyes shifting angrily.

"Hmmph! Money wasted."

Jane watched with pity in her heart as Paddy sought to prepare a party and create an air of joviality. She yearned to be more vocal, to be articulate, to say things that would lighten the dark atmosphere. Even the whisky that Paddy brought out didn't help, although they all had some—Paddy and his mother taking it neat, and Jane taking it with water. She would rather have had a glass of stout, but she hesitated to ask for anything that might cause difficulty in the getting. She had long ago learned to take what came, and it had helped in the house. She managed at last to blurt out several compliments about the brown bread, but it was Paddy who responded to her. She was grateful when it was over and they were able to get to the alphabet and the tracing of letters. She made an excuse and went into her bedroom early, having sat on the toilet longer than necessary simply to use up time. She undressed quickly, doused the lamp and lay flat on her back staring at the ceiling.

She started to doze but rising voices in the kitchen brought her swiftly awake. She couldn't make out the words, but the strident whine that she had heard when Mrs. Madigan talked to herself came again and again. She could catch little of Paddy's tone but she divined that he was seeking to calm his mother and to give only soft answers. She covered her ears so she wouldn't hear and when he came in at last, she pretended to be asleep. She liked to watch him undress, loved his presence, but she kept her eyes closed. She heard his shoes drop, and a click told her he had hung up his trousers. He was somehow neater than she, and she was striving to match him. Another sound baffled her for a minute, until she realized that he was on his knees praying beside the bed. It brought her to her own prayers, newly learned, and she began slowly to go through the Our Father. She had come to "as we forgive those. . ." when she slept.

She had no idea what time it was when a pounding on their door awoke her. Paddy was already sitting up in bed. Shouts were coming from the kichen as the pounding increased. A new sense of terror gripped her. It was Mrs. Madigan, in the middle of the night, but such was the mixture of shouts and whines that she could not be sure there were not two persons in the kitchen.

Then she distinctly heard Mrs. Madigan at the door, pounding and shouting. "Stop those filthy noises in there," she shouted. Thump! Thump! Thump! Thump! "Stop those filthy noises, the two of you." The thumping now became a sharp banging, as if she had taken up some instrument or a weapon. Jane remembered the knife trembling in her hands preparing the lunch. Paddy jumped from the bed and was putting on his trousers. The noises in the kitchen changed and multiplied. Dishes, pots and pans were being thrown about and the words that were shouted seemed no more than animal cries.

"I'm coming, Ma," Paddy shouted, lunging toward the door. When he opened it Jane jumped from the bed, put on her boots without stockings and a cotton dress over her flannel nightgown. When she got to the kitchen, Paddy and his mother had run through the door into the yard. Her initial fright turned to concern for Paddy, and she ran after them. Shouts and the sound of a struggle led her groping to the stone cowshed through the darkness that at the minute locked away stars and moon. When she reached it her eyes had adjusted to the dark and she could see two figures wrestling on the ground in the muck and old dung, framed by the stone doorway. She couldn't tell which form was which, until at that moment the clouds, hurrying before the wind, split and moonlight showed her Paddy kneeling upon his mother, who was prone in the mud and writhing violently. In her left hand was the knife Jane had seen her wielding to butter the bread. Paddy had all he could do to keep that hand with the knife pinned to the ground. With the other hand she was stuffing something into her mouth.

"Money, Jane! She's eating money! For God's sake, take it out of her mouth or she'll choke." He seemed barely able to get the words out because of his exertions. Jane threw herself on the ground beside them, and seized Mrs. Madigan's right hand. It clutched a sheaf of pound notes which she had been trying to eat. Jane forced the hand away from the mouth, astounded at the strength of the woman, and then managed to take the notes, many of them torn, from the claw-like grasp.

"She's gone mad," Paddy said in tears. "She's gone mad." The struggle continued. At length Paddy managed to shake the knife from her left hand. Mrs. Madigan once again began to writhe with demonic vitality.

"Rope! Get rope, Jane. We'll have to tie her or she'll kill herself or us."

"Where? Where's rope?"

"Cut down the goddam clothes line!" He nodded toward the knife and she had difficulty finding it in the dark. Quickly she picked it up and left the shed. She thought as she ran that it was the first time she had ever heard Paddy swear. The time taken in cutting down the line seemed interminable.

As she ran back toward the shed, she could hear the shrieks of the old woman. "Fucking whores!" was the only phrase she caught, and she thought how she had heard such time and again from her father in his rages, but here it turned her blood cold, for the lunacy gave it a diabolic resonance.

The terror of the unknown came upon her and she was conscious of facing the irrational for the first time in her life, something quite different from hatred or rage.

"Her feet first," Paddy whispered, as if he were out of breath. "Tie her feet first." Ropes and knots were something Jane knew well and she was quick with the work despite the thrashing of the naked bunioned feet. She soon had the ropes around the ankles, looped and looped again and securely knotted.

"Good," Paddy said. "Now the left hand here." Jane bound it and pulled it behind the woman's back. Paddy took the rope from her and—still kneeling on his mother—brought her right hand behind her and trussed the two together. He then rose. Mrs. Madigan, bound though she was, was still struggling and thrashing about.

"I'm going to be sick," Paddy said. Jane knelt beside the woman and held her with both hands to try and still the turbulence, to reduce the thrashing. Behind her, outside the shed, she could hear her husband retching. When he returned he caught his mother up in his arms, and carried her into the house.

"I'll have to bicycle to the Sullivans' and telephone Dr. O'Brien," he said. "You'll have to guard her."

"Wash the muck from you first," said Jane. With additional cords they bound the woman to her bed. Her speech was now incomprehensible, and her writhing was reduced to irregular spasms.

"Hurry, Paddy! Hurry back! I'm terribly afraid."

"She can't get loose."

"She may die. I don't want to be alone with her if she dies."

"I'll hurry."

She saw him to the door and saw him off on his bicycle, a flashlight held in his hand. When she returned to the bedroom to sit beside the sick woman, she could tell by the stink that she had become incontinent. Unable to think what to do, she sat stolidly, and began with her eyes closed to repeat the prayers she had learned and to raise her heart in petition.

24

THE WIND GUSHING past his ears was like a human voice but it had taken on a nightmare quality. He wanted to close his ears to it and he wanted to douse his mind as one would douse a kerosene lamp, twist a switch and shut it down. But there was no chance of that; his mind boiled with images of his mother writhing in the muck, her maniacal strength, the pound notes in her mouth sticking out like a demon's tongue. He did not need to ask where the money came from; he knew now. He understood the hundreds of hints he had heard from people in the town over the years, and the remarks of his Uncle Francis. Even as he had taught Jane how to add and subtract, figures came into his head to tell him that the farm had made money year after year while his mother hoarded almost all of it, keeping them living like paupers. He had no conception of how much money there might be in the hole in the floor of the storage barn which he would never have found if she had not disclosed it in the course of their struggle. He remembered her own remark about "money," about someone or other being after it, the priests, and he recalled the mention of money she had made the day she had begged him to come back.

The wind could not wash away the disgusting shout his mother had given at their bedroom door, and then his thoughts turned to fear for Jane. If his mother in her lunacy slipped the ropes with which she was bound, she could kill Jane. He felt a chill inside him, a chill of terror, the terror of the unknown, of the irrational.

He had come at last to the Sullivan gate. He leaped from his bicycle and vaulted the iron gate and ran up the walk. In response to his pounding, Michael Sullivan thrust his head from an upper window. "What is it? Is it you, Paddy?"

"My mother," Paddy said with brutal innocence, "has gone mad. Get Dr. O'Brien."

The head disappeared and the window went down. Paddy turned to go back. He was half way down the walk when the door opened and light flooded the walk. Eithne called to him. "Wait, Paddy!" He turned back. "Michael's phoning now. But isn't there something we can do?"

He put both his hands to his head. "I'm worried for Jane," he said. "She's alone with her this minute. I should have sent her here."

"Go along! Go along!" Eithne said. "We'll be right over."

He ran down the walk, opened and closed the gate and mounting his bicycle started back, plagued again by sickening images now that the mindless pedaling of the bicycle left his mind free. At the stone barn, he stopped long enough to conceal the loose money in the hole and replace the stone lid that had hidden the cache. He made no attempt to guess at the amount of money. He thought again of his mother trying to eat it, and he felt the same queasiness in his stomach that earlier had made him vomit. When he entered the kitchen he could see Jane in the bedroom sitting quietly in a chair with a rosary in her hands. He felt relief swell up in him.

At the sink, he washed his hands, took a drink of water, leaned with his hands against the sink to gather his thoughts and quiet his emotions. Somewhat composed he walked into the bedroom. On the bed where he had slept so many nights, so many years, his mother was still twitching in involuntary spasms, followed on occasion by sudden determined lurches. Although she moaned at times, she said nothing that was intelligible. The room stank, making Paddy cringe. He made a grimace at Jane to indicate his distress at the condition of the bed and the patient.

"I was waiting for you," Jane said. "I was afraid I might startle her if I tried to do anything."

He checked the cords that bound the woman's hands and feet and the others that held her to the bedstead.

"Come," he said, "I'll make you a cup of tea. She'll be all right until the doctor comes."

They went into the kitchen together but were there only minutes before the Sullivans came in. Paddy told them the story, omitting the words his mother had shouted at the door of the bedroom, and omitting the mention of the money in her mouth. After greeting the Sullivans, whom she had never seen together, Jane sat in silence, her rosary now in a pocket of the dress she had put on in his absence to replace the one marked by filth from the cowshed floor.

She rose to take over from Paddy to make and serve the tea, and suggested to him that he change his clothes. He looked suddenly at his clothes as if he had not noticed them before and went off to their bedroom.

"It's a tragedy," said Michael reflectively. "Could we say we saw it coming? Can't we say we saw it coming?" No one answered.

Eithne with her teacup in hand went into the bedroom but came out quickly. "Can't we get her cleaned up before the doctor comes?"

"Sure, we're afraid to untie her until she's been given something to quiet her like," Paddy called from the bedroom. Then he emerged newly dressed with his soiled clothes in his hands.

They had not long to wait. Dr. O'Brien came in, wearing khaki slacks and a jumper, carrying her black bag, her hair covered with a kerchief. After Paddy recited to her the night's events, the three women went into the room together. The doctor emerged after a minute or two.

"I've given her a needle," she said. "She'll be quiet now and we can wash and dress her."

Paddy sat with his head in his hands, listening to Michael. "God knows you were a good son to her, Paddy. Over the years you gave her no trouble. But she was a troubled woman, she's always been a troubled woman."

The voice came and went in his ears. But a smaller voice was in his head. It was his marriage that had set her off. They had been too close all those years, although he had never thought of it that way. She had found no comfort in prayer. From his early years he could remember her tirades against the priests. Where had that come from? His father had been a devout man. Meek. Like himself. Oh, without spunk. A coward. How stupid he had been. She had never shown him bills, or let him pay major ones. Maybe if she had had a doctor years ago, one that helped minds, she might have been cured and not be raving now. Oh, God, if he could only turn the years back and have her well, he would forgive her all her ranting and all her deceit. And yet, he thought, I'm only sorry for myself, enduring all this, the suffering and the shame. He was roused by a summons from Dr. O'Brien. He went into the bedroom where she had called.

"Now," she began, "I think we'll still have to keep her restrained until the morning and then we can get her over to St. Finian's. If there's anything that can be done for her, they're the ones who can do it." Paddy nodded. "But, Paddy," she continued, "I don't think she'll ever come back to the farm."

He had no tears left or he would have shed them. He half sobbed, nodded again dumbly and put his arm around Jane's shoulders. He drew in a long breath. "I blame myself," he said.

"That is nonsense," said Dr. O'Brien briskly, "utter nonsense. No one is to blame in these cases. It can be diet; it can be in the genes; it can be the damnable isolation of these god-forsaken farms. Forget the self-pity, the self-condemnation; it is only self-indulgence. Thank God you've got Jane to keep you and the farm going and to keep each other sane."

They both walked with her to her sedan. Michael Sullivan was carrying the soiled clothes to the incinerator, and Eithne was washing others at the sink.

"I'll be back in the morning. I have another call as it happens. You were fortunate to catch me or I'd stay with you here. I'll be back early in the morning. Get some sleep yourselves."

Paddy alone watched her huddle behind the wheel, turn the sedan around, and head back up the boreen. When he reentered the kitchen he found Jane in tears, seated on a chair with Eithne holding her head.

"It's been a dreadful strain on her," Eithne said.

"It has," said Paddy. "It will be with us for a long while."

Jane suddenly sat erect, a look of fright in her blue eye. "Och," she cried, "it's the curse that's on the tinkers." Her distress was so evident that Eithne was taken aback and stepped away from her for a second. Paddy leaped forward and gripped her by the shoulders and shook her violently.

"That's the worse nonsense of all," he shouted. "That's crazy talk." Then, kneeling to embrace her, he said: "Forgive me. I should never have used that word." The two of them wept together.

The Sullivans stood and watched for a minute until after a nod from Eithne, Michael stepped forward and brought Paddy to his feet. "Come now," he said, "you are both overwrought. Let's have a touch of whisky here and a moment's rest and then we'll go to bed for what's left of the night."

Paddy faced them rubbing his eyes, sensing within him the struggle between the boy and the man. "I'm sorry," he said, "I forgot my manners. Michael's right. For God's sake, let us have a drink to the living, to those of us who are here and well."

25

THEY SET OUT for Killarney that noon in Father Curtin's automobile, Paddy beside him in the front seat. In the rear seat, Mrs. Madigan, her arms bound to her sides, was flanked by Sergeant Callaghan and Dr. O'Brien. Jane, exhausted after a night without sleep and having toiled with Dr. O'Brien and Mrs. McCann to wash and dress again the sick woman, had watched them go. Paddy's love for her welled up in him as he thought of her attention to his mother, and he marveled at the strength in his mother's withered limbs. Their combined strength had been needed to bind her to the bed. He relived the night as they drove along, and the events of the morning. He had gone to the barn to cover with muck again the stone that covered the cache. When the others arrived for the hospital trip, he moved as in a funk, content to let others take charge and give the orders. He would have preferred to remain behind with Jane, but knew that his duty lay elsewhere.

"I've telephoned Killarney," the sergeant said. "They're expecting us."

Father Curtin murmured an acknowledgement but no

one else spoke. Paddy sensed that they were all reluctant to do or say anything that might arouse his mother from her stupor. The drug was wearing off, and they were scarcely past the village, a matter of seven miles, when she began to rant again and writhe. Dr. O'Brien tried to quiet her and was almost succeeding when Paddy turned to look at her and their eyes met.

She screamed. "There he is and the devil from hell beside him!"

"It's all right, Ma," he said, "it's all right. Everything will be all right."

He felt his voice crack, and a sense of nightmare and helplessness came over him. Her eyes, which had been glaring at him, now looked beyond, as if focusing on something else, something unearthly, and unseen by any save her. Even as he watched her, her face seemed to change, and he hardly recognized the enraged eyes, the purple face, and the contorted lips, pursing and then pulling back over the strong brown teeth.

"The whores of hell have him. They have him. Get him away from me!"

The voice rose in a tempest of lunatic strength so as to frighten him. Father Curtin, seeing the woman struggling, pulled the sedan to the side of the road. Sergeant Callaghan and Dr. O'Brien had hold of her and were trying to stop the writhing.

"Paddy," Father Curtin said, "I think if you leave the car. . . She's terribly disturbed—it might make a difference."

Tormented and sick at heart, Paddy opened the door and stepped out. He saw the priest wave at him to get out of sight and he walked to the rear of the automobile. Through the rear window he could see the tumult in the woman slowly subside, her passion evidently diminishing. Father Curtin was suddenly beside him.

"I think for her personal safety and your own peace of mind. . ."

"I can't," Paddy interrupted.

"Paddy, there is nothing you can do that we cannot. Your presence disturbs her. The doctor doesn't want to sedate her again. Let us go on with her. You mustn't blame yourself. We'll take her to St. Finian's and you turn back. When she's settled there, I'll drive you over. It's not safe for any of us to have her take these seizures in the car."

Paddy could not answer. Tears ran down his cheeks. Unable to stop them, he hung his head.

"Believe me, Paddy, it's for the best."

Paddy nodded. He took a deep breath and looked out toward the river that ran beside the highway.

"I'll beg a lift," he said. "I'll try to follow along."

"Stay on the main road," Father Curtin said. "It may be we'll catch you on the way back."

Paddy stared at the river.

"However," the priest said firmly, "I do think you would do better to go home." He put his hand on Paddy's shoulder. "Get some rest and be prepared for tomorrow. You have a job you have to answer for and you have the farm."

Paddy nodded again.

"Go along, father," he said, "and thank you."

"These things take time, Paddy. Be patient. The Lord has his reasons."

The priest turned, got back into the sedan and drove off. Paddy stood for a long time by the side of the road. He started to walk back the way they had come, but then halted and leaned against a stone wall. Terrible visions of his mother lying in the muck on the floor of the shed, gasping on the bed under the bonds he had tied, glaring at him in the automobile, made him pull his tight fists close to his chest and then cast them out as if flinging evil away from him. He decided to follow to the hospital. He must go. It was his responsibility. He moved to the side of the road and began to gesture at each car that came along. The third one stopped, and he ran to it and opened the door. The driver was a stranger to him, a harried-looking salesman with samples and folders all over the rear seat and small cardboard boxes beside him on the front seat.

"Thanks for stopping," said Paddy.

"Thanks for sure," he said. "You're welcome. I'm going to Kenmare."

It was on the way. Paddy was relieved that the man did not seem eager to talk and so he himself said nothing, wondering with throbbing head just where on the road the priest's car might be with its tragic burden. The ride to Kenmare to him seemed interminable, but at length he alighted outside the main street of Kenmare where the road turned left for Killarney. As he started along toward Killarney, the rain came, a torrential downpour. He fled to a pub to sit out the storm—wet, discouraged and of two minds. Father Curtin had told him to go home, but the remnant of an ancient fear that had brought him this far was tugging at him to continue on.

Other travelers had followed his lead out of the rain and the pub had become crowded just as he began to sip on the glass of stout he had ordered. He stood at the corner of the bar near a window and the door, watching the rain through the smoke-smutted pane, weary from the lack of sleep, strung out emotionally. If he waited long enough they would be starting back and would find him on the long road. He dawdled over his drink, saw Jane waving him a sorrowful goodbye, relived again the horror of the night, saw his mother pounding on the door, saw her prone in the filth of the shed, saw her chewing the banknotes.

He prayed for the rain to stop, determined at one moment to turn homeward and in the next to go on to the hospital. His mind was made up as he finished his drink. He would head for home. If they overtook him and picked him up, grand. If he was offered a lift he would take it and be home before them. He had twenty miles to go. On his bicycle he would not have minded it.

26

AFTER TWO HOURS of work, she made herself a pot of tea and buttered a scone; but she couldn't eat. The memory of the whole night affair was too rank in her mind, and although her uneasiness had fled, a shadow of despondency had descended on her. She sat dreaming of the seashore and a boat and felt herself half dozing, sailing away into the air on a boat like a swan out of some story her mother had told her when she was a little girl.

She heard the clop of a horse's hooves but paid no attention until she heard a step in the barnyard and she leaped to her feet in elation. She had not expected Paddy back so soon; had she been asleep at the table? No, it was bright sunshine at the door. And why a horse? She started for the door when her father walked in.

"Well," he said, sneering, "ain't ye quite the lady." She was stunned and bewildered. She had not thought of him since two days before and never dreamed of his returning to Sneem.

"Da!" she cried. "The gardai will be after you."

"No fear of that," he said. "Never you fear."

She stood at the table, with terror growing inside her like a small seed slowly bursting and magnifying itself into a sprouting evil plant.

"Haven't you got a kiss for your old Da?"

He had a long piece of cord in his hands which he kept twisting and untwisting. She thought he might lash her, but he made no move toward her.

"Will you have some tea?"

"Tea, is it? I'll have some whisky. Have you a drop of that around?"

She was conscious that he had already been drinking.

"Sit down," she said. "I'll get it."

She went to the small cabinet where the bottles were kept and brought one forth with a tumbler. She started to pour out a mouthful with a shaking hand, but he snatched the bottle from her and all but filled the tumbler.

"Mrs. High and Mighty Madigan."

He emptied half the glass, gasped a bit, and put it down on the table. She had never seen him more disheveled. His hair was uncut and filthy with chunks of mud visible in it. His face was smeared with dirt and stained with dried blood. He wore ragged trousers and a jacket she had never seen before, the cuffs of it greasy with dried oil, and he had no shirt except an undershirt. His blue eyes were bloodshot and one of them watered steadily.

"Let me. . ." she began. "Let me wipe that blood off your forehead and cheek."

He said nothing but watched her wet a towel and come to him and start to wash the dirt away. Before she realized what was happening, he had both her wrists bound with the cord from his lap and her attempt to wrench backwards only tightened the slip knot on her joined wrists, one tied over the other. He was on his feet now and had lashed the wrists tightly together and was dragging her across the kitchen floor. He threw the cord over an iron hook high on the wall beside the door of the bedroom. Despite her struggling and her strength, she found her resistance won her nothing. He hoisted her until she was hanging with the tips of her shoes barely touching the floor. She made no sound during the struggle after the first gasp of surprise. He turned back to the table and sat down to his drink, gazing at her with alternating sneers and drunken grins.

"Now, Janie," he said, "just tell me where the money is and I'll be off on my roan."

She looked at him for a full minute and then said slowly, "There's no money in this house. There may be a pound or two in my purse."

"And where is that?"

"In the room behind me."

"We'll check in a minute."

He poured himself another tumbler of whisky.

"Ye never were a truthful girl, Jane," he said mockingly. "And ye may be lying to me now. We'll see. We'll see."

"Let me down."

"Time enough for that. We must settle the money question."

He sat sullenly drinking and then hurled the empty glass across at the sink where it shattered against the brass faucet. He took a swig from the bottle. After wiping his mouth on his greasy cuff, he arose unsteadily. He walked across the kitchen and went into the bedroom behind her. She could hear him pulling the bureau drawers onto the floor and rummaging about. He came out after several minutes with the pocketbook that Dr. O'Brien had given her as a wedding gift. At the table he sat examining the contents—a lace handkerchief, a lipstick she had never used, a compact with face powder, eye drops for her bad eye, a set of rosary beads from the curate, and a small change purse. Having pushed the casual items to the back of the table against the wall, he opened the change purse, and took out three pounds and some coins.

"Bedamn," he said, "that's better than half a quid. Ye'll remember I used to beat ye if ye came back with less than half a quid." He chuckled, coughed and half choked and then spat on the floor.

She said nothing. Her wrists stung, and she wondered what she would have to do to get rid of him.

"Paddy and the garda will soon be back," she said. "You had better cut me down and take the money and go." He laughed and looked at her slyly out of the corner of his eye.

"They'll be a long time getting back from the asylum," he said. "A long, long time, Janie, and no mistake about that. Ye see, I know a good bit about what's going on."

"If they catch you, you'll pay dearly."

"Now then," he said, "we must get to business. Where's the old lady's hoard?"

Oh, God, she thought, how much does he know?

"Hoard?"

"Everyone in Sneem knew she had a hoard, except her stupid son. But ye must have found it by now. Yer not that stupid, Janie."

She turned over in her mind what to say.

"I swear to God there's no hoard in this house."

"Maybe it's under the floor then."

He staggered more than walked over and faced her. Suddenly he grabbed the throat of her blouse and ripped it down the front and half off her.

"Now then," he said, "just how far do you want me to go?"

She made no answer.

"It's all up to yer ladyshit."

He threw his head back and laughed at his own slip of the tongue.

"Ladyshit is right," he cried. "Yer ladyshit. It's true spoken for you, Mike Ward."

He reeled backwards and went again to the table and drank from the bottle. He stood facing the wall drinking and then turned with alarming suddenness and dashed toward her. Grasping her skirt, he tore it from her and then seized her underpants and garter belt and pulled them down to her ankles, trying to get them over her boots. He fell down in the failed effort, picked himself up slowly and unsteadily and stared at her.

"There you are now in the height of fashion, yer ladyshit, with your cunty showing."

Involuntarily, all the years of hatred swelling inside her, she spat at him. He was too far out of reach and merely laughed at her. He wandered out of the kitchen and into the room where she had just washed the floor. She heard him throwing things around, upsetting the bed, kicking in the side of something and cursing to himself. She tried to twist her hands somewhat but the effort only made the cords cut her wrists. She thought she could swing her feet to a nearby chair but it was out of reach. It was hopeless. She was too enraged to cry out. She thought for a moment of telling where some of the money was to get rid of him; if it had been hers she would have, giving him enough to end her suffering. But it was Paddy's money; she would rather suffer. She could bear a lot of that; she had borne it before, and she was stronger now against him than she had ever been. She had a home and a life of her own. He came back into the kitchen as she was trying once again to reach the chair.

"Ye needn't make it worse for yerself," he said. "Just tell yer Da where the money is."

"There's no money, you fool." She had never called him worse.

"I'll have a look in the loft." Before he started up the ladder steps in the corner that led to the loft she had never seen herself, he went to the cabinet that held the bottled goods. He found a bottle half filled with a liqueur and taking another tumbler filled it. The portion emptied the bottle and he flung it in a corner. He drank half of it in two swallows and then started for the ladder. In passing, he tugged at her brassiere. It didn't break but slipped off one breast and caught beneath it. She spat at him again, this time striking his shoulder. Despite his increasing unsteadiness he scrambled quickly up the ladder stairs, thrust open the trap and disappeared. She could hear his steps above her and the sound of more rummaging.

She felt certain now he would try to rape her, and she practiced bringing her knees up sharply. She found she could do so despite the pain in her wrists. One of them was bleeding. What a fool she had been to think that his step was Paddy's. Paddy would not be back until late—late, late. She stopped thinking about it and hung in agony. She couldn't finish any of the prayers she had learned.

Her father came down from the loft, and stood before her opening his fly. Although he fingered himself for a long time, in his drunkenness it was to no avail, and he went for the liqueur left in the glass. Tottering backwards a step or two he put his hand on the stove to steady himself and yelped in pain. Rubbing his hand, he put it into a pan of water in the sink, and holding the glass in his left hand, he withdrew his right hand from the water and put it under his left arm. Turning back, he sat down again at the table.

He drank the remaining liqueur slowly and almost as soon as it was finished, fell asleep in the chair. She felt her prayers had been answered. Hanging in her agony, she tried to put herself into a trance where the pain would be something far off, happening to someone else. She couldn't tell how long he slept. The clock was ticking behind her, but she couldn't even guess at the time.

When he awoke it was late afternoon; the sun had moved from the open door. His bleary eyes focussed on her and, after staring a while, he sprang to his feet.

"Where's the money, ye dirty tinker bitch?"

She shook her head.

He looked at his blistered hand and then at the stove. Moving over to it, he took the lid lifter and removing a lid thrust the lifter into the glowing turf. She watched him now with a new terror in her heart. The process, it seemed, was too slow to suit him and he spat on the other lid and the sound of the sizzling of the spit filled the room. He took the lid-lifter and carefully raised the hot lid from the stove, carrying it unsteadily before him.

"Let's see where the money is."

His speech was slurred, all but incomprehensible. He brought the hot lid slowly toward her bared belly, evidently intent on pressing the edge of it against her. He thrust it against her. She screamed, brought up her knees in frantic effort, and knocked the lid and the holder from his hands. He fell backwards on the floor, cursing, but the hot lid falling from his hands struck her naked thigh and she screamed a second time in pain. The thigh burn was much larger than the burn on her abdomen. She watched him as he started to recover awkwardly and began to rise when Paddy rushed through the door.

Shoving the half-risen man aside so that he fell again sprawling, Paddy caught her in his arms and lifted her high in the air so that with the help of a gesture of her arms, the rope came off the hook. He set her on the chair and reached to untie the ends of the rope. She leaned half against the back of the chair and against the wall, moaning. He had to use a knife to get the cord off her wrists.

"Jane, oh, my God—Jane, what was he doing to you?"

"Paddy, oh God bless you, Paddy. You came."

He was carrying her in his arms toward the bedroom, turning sideways to get her through the door, and placed her gently on top of the quilt.

"He was after the money, Paddy!"

"Your wrists," he said. "Your wrists."

"I said there was none in the house."

"Your wrists—my God, your wrists and your thigh."

"I'm all right. I'm burned but I'm all right."

"Where else? Oh, Jesus, I see. I see. Poor child. Poor you."

"Kiss me. Paddy."

Her eyes closed as he kissed her and he was afraid she had fainted but they opened quickly, one dead in its socket, the other alive with pain.

"He may come back after you, Paddy. Be careful."

But her father had fled the house.

27

"DO YOU FIND me changed?" he asked her suddenly, a question for which in their walking back from mass there had been no preparation. She turned her good eye up at him and frowned.

"Now, isn't that the odd question to be asking?" she said, making the import of her own question obvious by her inflection.

"Father Curtin says I have changed. He says I'm older and more brooding."

"Ah, Paddy," she said, "it's all behind us. Put it out of your mind."

He had been unable to do that. He had a mind full of hate and a lust for revenge. Two months had passed and the autumn was upon them, the land golden with gorse, and the fields still so green that the sky seemed to reflect it. In the confessional he had told Father Curtin how disturbed he was and how he hated his father-in-law.

"Hate is a consuming passion, a sin," Father Curtin told him. "You can drown in it, just as your mother, Paddy, drowned in her own bitterness. Leave him to God, Paddy, and leave him to the law."

The vision of his mother writhing in the filth of the floor of the shed which used to torment him had been replaced by the sight of his wife hanging, naked and humiliated, in the kitchen of their home. Her wrists were only now healing, for the cords had cut to the bone and the wound yielded to the ministrations of Dr. O'Brien more slowly than the burns on her belly and thigh.

He had listened with horror to her account of her ordeal with her father, demanding every detail, but time and again having to put his hand over her mouth to stop her talking. He could not bear to listen, and yet he saw himself obliged in the role of judge to evaluate the evidence before he passed sentence. When she told him how her father had stripped her bra from her, Paddy walked to the side of the road and looked off in the distance.

"He's a monster," he said, returning to her side.

"But you want to hear."

"Tell me no more."

A minute later, he had to ask her to continue. He was very conscious that it bothered him more to listen than for her to suffer through it again. She was forgiving to the point of complacency, so that he rocked from side to side in anguish, unable to match her forbearance. In all, it took him three days before he had heard the story entire. She had not told Dr. O'Brien as much and she had told Father Curtin even less, but both those friends knew from her wrists and the little they were told.

Paddy knew that what had happened had changed him; he had entered a world he had not known existed. He had become a man, he knew; but he also knew he was not sure that he wanted to be that kind of man, a man with iron in his heart, a man he did not know how to deal with, a man who seemed not entirely under his own control. He had suddenly taken a grip on the world, or the world had taken a grip on him, and it was a world he wanted to destroy. At the heart of things lay a canker. He became a brooding man; a man with a bent and baffled purpose; an unhappy man where he could not have been unhappy before. The center of the great disc of contentment eluded him. Where he had wept before, he raged now.

He had at first tried to hide his brooding from her and thought he had succeeded because she seemed happy enough. The curate had come and blessed the house to dissipate whatever breath of evil lingered in it. They had spent a good deal of the money to have it cleaned and painted, to put down flooring and buy electric heaters for the bedroom and to supply hot water. His obsession soured the pleasure for him, but he pretended a delight at what they did, and at the brightness of the house. They had bought two bicycles and were planning the purchase of a small truck for the farm. The amount of money his mother had hidden away stunned him and he had taken the matter up with Father Curtin. He felt the money might be cursed and should be given away. The priest waved aside his fears.

"Do not fret about it," he said. "Farm and money are legally yours. Do with it as you like. There is no curse on it. It is money your mother deprived you of over the years. Spend it wisely. I know you too well to have to tell you not to yield to senseless extravagance."

But the enjoyment was closed to him by the visions in his mind of Jane's ordeal, the obscenities of Ward and his escape. Day after day he expected the garda to report that the man had been taken, one place or another, perhaps in England. But no word came. In one corner of his mind, the thought came and went that Ward would return, perhaps to try to kill him or abuse and kill Jane. It made him reluctant to stay away from home any length of time. He stopped visiting his mother in the hospital; the authorities there had asked him to. They would tell him when he should come. True to his word, he continued to give Mulcahy three days a week for the month that followed the assault on Jane, and he waited for his release so that he could turn his full attention to the farm.

She who had suffered so, who had been so debased, who had seen her father at his worst, a man deteriorated past degradation into the heart of evil—she, Paddy saw, seemed untroubled by her ordeal.

"There are people, Paddy," Father Curtin said to him when he remarked on her stolidity, "that evil cannot touch." The priest leaned forward in the confessional box, almost looking directly at Paddy instead of holding his head sideways as he customarily did. "What such people have found is something close to sanctity." Paddy thought of that now as they passed the line of holly trees and crossed the brook on stepping stones. He heard her words inside him again: "It's all behind us." He couldn't answer her without letting her know that it was not all behind him but very much in him.

He was waiting for a day he knew would come. If they had brought him word that Mike Ward had been found dead on the road, or drowned in the bogs or the river, or found, as his roan had been found, with her leg broken so that she had to be destroyed, he would have felt cheated. He was owed something: the moment when he could repay filthy violence with the cleansing hands of justice. Justice is mine sayeth the

Lord, but a voice told him there are times when a man is the instrument of God's justice. He didn't dare hint at his thoughts to Jane. In the confessional he listened docilely to the admonitions of Father Curtin, but he could not yield to the logic. His sinfulness—for he recognized his hatred as such—troubled him, and one Sunday he had started for Communion and turned back in the aisle, admittedly unworthy. Fortunately for his sanity, the farm work absorbed him.

Mulcahy, mopping his fat face with his large bandanna, at last released him from his oral contract, and bade him Godspeed with many a minatory word. For the next month he had worked his own farm morning and evening with Jane, in what should have been a blissful summer idyll. For her it certainly seemed so as she sang about the house, learned to read, and spent the evenings close beside him, when they were not walking to the shore, reading one of the newspapers he bought in the village and which was used as her textbook. Occasionally during such moments he would feel himself at the center of his great circle of contentment but time and again, some drama on the radio, some story in the newspaper, or a mere gesture of her arm with its scarred wrist, would bring the iron of gloom and hatred back into his mind. It prevented him from enjoying the profitability of the work on the farm which rose beyond his calculation, and he had to pay a solicitor to instruct him in matters of business dealings. He began to read the business pages of the newspapers with avidity.

One night he read that the pub in Castle Cove, the small neighboring village, had been robbed, liquor taken and an attempt made on the cash drawer. His whole body came atingle. He put the paper down and walked out into the waning light of the evening and thought of Mike Ward and where he might camp or hide out with the garda after him, and a price on his head. He turned and studied the hillside across the highway from him where the caravan had stood. There would be no caravan; perhaps a horse. But if Ward came the countryside would show a sign. Paddy could name every house on the road and identify every coil of smoke he saw rising against the green mountains, mounting from the turf fires in a dozen hearths.

Each night took him to the vantage point from which he could count the spirals of smoke, noting the occasional absence of one or the other, looking for one that didn't belong in that quiet rural landscape. Two ruins stood far up the hill opposite the Madigan farm, but Paddy knew Ward would not hide out in either, although many tinkers had used them in the past. Either one was too likely a spot for a criminal to hide in the Kerry countryside. Even as he walked along with Jane, his eyes would search the hillside first, and then the shoreline and then return to the hills.

It was he now who fell taciturn and she who talked. He listened to her read the newspaper aloud, waiting for the second clue he knew would come. A second theft, again of food and liquor! He started to take the paper from her hands, and she looked surprised at his motion. A man had entered a grocery store between Sneem and Castle Cove and had beaten the woman shopkeeper into insensibility. Paddy's intuition became a certainty for him, even though he was wise enough to know that it was his intense desire for revenge that confirmed his judgment.

Three nights later in the descending dusk, very late in the evening, he saw a thread of smoke rising against the dark green of the hills, a thread of smoke that had no origin he could name, a thread of smoke from an unknown source, all the more suspicious because it came onto the landscape so late in the evening, an hour when one was not likely to notice unless they were especially watching, an hour when the garda were at home. Knowing that his prey was near—for he so considered Ward—he calculated in his mind where the fire might be that would be raising the twisting smoke, pencil thin in the dusk. He stood so long, so still, surveying the hills, starting and stopping in his pacing, that Jane came out and stood watching him as he stared into space.

"You're very quiet," she said.

"'Tis nothing," he answered. "It is just that the still of the evening brings a stillness into a man's heart." He turned and went in with her but he knew. Mike Ward was hiding in Staigue Fort, a construction of the megalithic age, half as old as time, a mile and more up the hillside. Beyond reach of the automobile except when a determined effort was made to get there, the last two hundred yards had to be on foot.

It was a magnificent circle of stone, built before Stonehenge and preserved through the centuries by its inaccessibility. Within it were half a dozen subterranean chambers where a man might sleep unobserved. Not fifty persons a year made their way to it. From it, to either side and beyond, a fugitive might slip into the woods and never be seen, pursued only on foot by the most dedicated of law enforcers. Moved by an inner conviction that spurned logic, Paddy made his plans to besiege the fort, to stalk his man, to wait and watch and strike.

His impatience overmatched his cunning. He set out the next day. He took his bicycle, made an excuse to Jane about the sale of bullocks, and, putting on his heaviest boots, he started for the fort.

"Will you be back for lunch?" she asked. "You're taking nothing with you."

"I hope to be back," he said, "but if I am not you take yours and do not fret about me. I'll be back in God's good time."

As he pedaled off, he saw Father Curtin's sedan head up Mulcahy's drive.

28

THE RAIN BEGAN as he reached the turn to take him up the hill to the ancient Staigue fort, a circular stronghold out of the Iron Age, built of earth and dry stone without mortar, thirty feet high in some spots, dipping to ten in others because of the centuries of erosion, a barred gate the only entrance. Although the rain was heavy at the start, it diminished in force as he went along. When he reached the iron gate of the fort, having walked his bicycle over the last stretch of stony ground, he found the gate, customarily unlatched to receive the occasional tourist, bolted on the inside. His sense of excitement increased, for only someone hiding within would slip a wedge of wood or iron into the iron cups. He stepped back from the gate and began to climb the wall. The flat stones, piled without mortar, but bearing soil and some vegetation brought on the wind over the centuries, offered fairly easy but slippery climbing. He was only half way up when he saw Ward peering down at him.

"Get the hell out of here or I'll crush your bloody skull with a slab of stone!" Ward shouted. He threw a large stone down at Paddy, striking him a glancing blow on the left shoulder. Paddy leaped back to the ground. Without a word he sprinted around the base of the wall, familiar to him from boyhood, and came to a spot where he knew the top of the wall would be more easily reached because of an accumulation of soil against the western side. He knew too that Ward, running on top of the wall, which gave very jagged footing, could not move as quickly as he. He came to the low climb, scaled the wall, and was standing on it when the tinker arrived, a stone in either hand, as primordial as the fort itself, a cave man out of a primitive past. Paddy saw him as the savage he was, a brute figure from the misty aeons when human sacrifice was celebrated as regularly as the mass today, and the cruel violation of woman and child was common. His hatred for the man surged through him, stimulating his blood and nerves, and rousing a sense of vengeance that tightened his sinews and moved his muscles without his will.

"Ward," he said, "I've come to kill you!"

The man responded by hurling a large rock at him with his right hand and rushing at him with his left hand held high, gripping a sharply-pointed rock shaped like a dagger, like a horn about his head. Paddy easily dodged the first stone thrown at him. The wall, less than ten feet wide with treacherous footing of loose stones, still wet from the rain, offered little space to sidestep or dodge, and the left-handed blow from Ward caught Paddy's jacket on the right side and his upper arm felt the blow.

Ward was taller than Paddy, quick and powerful, but Paddy's rage—he sensed it himself—gave him the maniacal strength he had seen in his mother. He wrenched the dagger-stone from Ward's grasp and then brought his left hand up in a sharp blow to the tinker's head. Ward turned and ran, scrambling over the loose stones on top of the wall. Paddy picked up a large stone and flung it at the fleeing man. It struck him in the back so that he fell forward on his hands and knees. Before Paddy could overtake him, though, he had risen and leaped from the wall to the soft grass of the enclosure. Paddy jumped after him and could feel his ankle turn on the wet grass. He had been surprised at Ward's strength, and was surprised now by his fleetness. Paddy knew that if he didn't close with the man quickly, he could escape. Ward had struggled to his feet and was standing as if undecided whether to fight or flee, when Paddy sprang at him and brought him to the ground. They grappled on the grass, and for the second time, Ward began to speak, cursing Paddy, stringing out profanities Paddy hardly heard in the struggle. He said nothing himself, determined to conquer the man or die in the attempt. Let the tinker waste his breath in blasphemies.

They matched tensions of strength in an effort that left them momentarily locked like living statues. Paddy's arms ached like an abscessed tooth. Their breathing became more controlled, and the tinker snarled, "I'll sell her to you; I've sold her before."

The filth of the man electrified Paddy and intensified his rage. New strength surged through him. He rose to his feet, lifting Ward with him. Raising him above his head, he threw him to the ground, then leaped on the prostrate man and began to pummel body, face and head until he knew that Ward was insensible and that he had broken his own left hand.

Near exhaustion, he rose unsteadily to his feet and looked around him for a large stone. He walked to the wall, and seized one and returned, prepared to crush the filthy, battered head as it lay on the ground. The stone was black as death, and as heavy as the hatred in his heart. Staring down at the tinker, he wished he were conscious to see the blow that was coming. He paused for seconds, looking at the fallen man. He thought of going to the brook and getting water to revive him, then dismissed the thought. He raised the stone above his head, but, grunting angrily, turned aside and threw it on the ground. At that moment, into his mind came the vision of Jane hanging half naked in the kitchen, branded and ashamed, and he picked up the stone again and raised it on high.

"Paddy! Don't! Throw the stone away."

A strong male voice was calling from the top of the wall. He turned to see Father Curtin, bareheaded and leaping to the grass. Angrily, he held the stone above his head, and hesitated for the space of moment. But his body could not stop.

29

WHEN PADDY, RIDING off on his bicycle, had seen Father Curtin's car that morning, the priest was bringing the Blessed Sacrament to Mrs. Mulcahy, who was said to be dying. Mr. Mulcahy, mopping his moist pate with a large red bandanna, walked him back to his sedan parked on the crushed stone of the driveway beside the strung barbed wire fence.

"She doesn't seem much in pain," Father Curtin said.

"The prayers helped her," said the stout man. "Paddy came over the other night to say the rosary beside her with me. Sure there's nothing like the rosary, Father."

"How is he?"

"Who?"

"Paddy."

"He looked grand this morning, hurrying along toward Castle Cove."

And so the priest had driven over to the Madigan farm. As he motored up the boreen, he could see Jane piling hay, pitchfork in her hands, her movements easy and rhythmical.

"'Behold her solitary in the field,'" he recited aloud as he stopped the sedan, and, stepping into the roadway, he started across the field to her.

Seeing him approach, she stopped her work but did not advance. He raised the flat of his hand lest she do so, and called out a good morning and a blessing on her.

"You've come too late," she said in her soft voice.

"Too late?"

She nodded. "Too late. He's gone off to find my Da."

"Did he say so?"

She shook her head.

He looked down at the auburn hair and the mismatched eyes. He had seen burning pain in that eye before, the day in the church when he had sent her off with a few pounds and she had come running back to him.

"But are you sure?" he asked.

She nodded. "I'm sure." She hung her head. "Father, I know him."

"Do you know where your father is?"

She shook her head and wiped her eyes with the knuckles of both hands, the pitchfork resting against her.

"Ah, Father," she said, "he wouldna left if he didn't know. Haven't I watched him all these months studying and scanning the skyline and the hills for a sign? Something in the papers told him."

The woman in Waterville, he thought, beaten to insensibility in her shop and found dead the next day. An unusual crime, and one that Ward might well have committed. The Special Branch had been called in, and there was no doubt in his mind that Sergeant Callaghan had told them of Ward.

"He took his bicycle?" he asked, half to himself.

"He did."

He looked across the brown fields to the green hills

beyond, half of them a black green where the woods covered the slopes. A man could hide there for half a century unless the gardai brought in tracking dogs—and could starve to death in a month. Paddy had been cycling toward Castle Cove. Well, he would tell the gardai to get after him before he got himself in trouble.

"I'll have the gardai find him," he said. "I wouldn't want him to do something rash."

Tears welled in both her eyes. He took her face in his hands and kissed her on the top of her head. "Woman, woman," he said, "do not be troubled. Paddy'll soon be home."

"You've come too late," she said again, and turned to the hay.

To hide her tears, he told himself, and he found his guess confirmed as she began to shake with sobbing. Dropping the pitchfork, she threw herself into his arms.

"Oh," she cried out, "I have a child in me and he's gone."

"Jane, Jane," said the priest, trying to keep his voice from trembling. "Paddy will be back. Rejoice. REJOICE. Your child, your child. He'll not leave you and the child."

"He doesn't know," she said. "He'll do something dreadful and not come back."

The collie came across the field and began to nuzzle between them, envious of their affection. She stepped back from the priest and patted the dog.

"Jane," he said, picking up the pitchfork and passing it to her, "I'm delighted you are going to be a mother. Now, let's be clear about Paddy. He rode off on his bicycle, and that this morning, but didn't tell you where he was off to. Is that correct? Did he say when he would be back?"

She leaned on the pitchfork and took a long breath. "He said he'd be back for lunch. . ." Here her voice caught. ". . . or in God's good time."

The last phrase stirred the priest's nerves, rasping on them. The words bore an ominous undertone.

Finding Paddy, he now saw, could not wait upon notification to the gardai in Sneem; he must find him immediately. It was the thought of the child in her womb and the mention of time that made him think of Staigue Fort. He had always thought of the ancient fort as a titanic womb, harboring Time that was never born but stayed in the mysterious ring of rocks, dry-piled stones, like an invisible fetus, the culmination or termination of a civilization the very name of which was lost to scholars.

"I'll go look for him now," he said, and ran to his sedan. He drove recklessly along the boreen to the main road, turning left there in the path of an oncoming, rumbling, rubber-tired tractor so precariously that the driver, a tow-haired young farmer, hollered an obscenity at him. He laughed because of his dereliction and the rude response, but the laugh was brief and grim. He was soon turning into the road running up the hill to the fort. At the end of the paved section he drove on, despite the danger to his tires from the sharp pointed rocks, protruding here and there like the tips of javelins.

At length he had to abandon the car in the middle of the lane and sprint to the fort. He knew it well. The gate was bolted on the inside, as he expected it might be. Peering over it, he caught sight of two figures wrestling on the boggy grass. He ran to the spot where he knew the accumulated soil of centuries had risen close to the top of the wall. He was breathless when he reached it and his heart was pulsing painfully. He had to pause before he scaled the stone facade to the jagged flat surface of stones on top.

Below him, in the center of the ancient arena, he saw Paddy with a huge stone raised above his head, like a troglodyte from the century the fort was built, primordial in brutality, the inert figure of Ward lying before him.

"Drop the stone, Paddy!" he cried. "Throw it away, away!"

He was too late. She had been prescient. As he jumped, he saw the stone fall. He heard a dreadful thump, but then saw that the stone had missed the head and lay two feet away. Paddy stood in a slump, swaying slightly and raising his hands to his head. Father Curtin knelt beside the tinker and knew at once that the last blow had been unnecessary. The man was dead.

Instinctively, he began absolution over the corpse. The face was a bloody pulp from which one staring blue eye, the only identifiable feature left, glared at him in mockery: Evil rejoicing in breeding Evil. He thought of the man's daughter in the farm he had just left—life and the goodness of life breeding life.

He rose and looked about him. Paddy was gone. The gate was unbolted and open. He started toward it, and in his mind's eye saw the man fleeing and sensing the scourge of remorse. Once Paddy had heard him start the prayers, begin the final absolution, he had known that Ward was dead.

The priest raced toward the gate. "Paddy, come back! Jane is pregnant! The gardai will be wanting Ward for murder in Waterville!"

But he knew how ominous the situation was. Paddy would not go back to his home.

30

SHE SAT IN the doorway in the failing sun, watching the black sedan come along the boreen, pausing to let Sullivan's cows surge like a black and white sea around and past it, their tails lashing off the flies she knew were there. She sensed what news the priest would bring and dreaded it. All day she had worked in the fields, not merely to get the chores done for the day but to let the physical motion tire her and the fingers of detail keep her mind off what she feared in her heart might have happened.

"You're too late," she had told the priest. The words swung in her head like a cow bell, "Too late, too late, too late." She hoped he had not felt it as a rebuke. For it was she who had been too late. It was she alone who could have stopped Paddy from setting forth to disaster. If only she had told him that she was alive within, that she was pregnant, that he was to be a father, that the farm was to have a produce that would laugh, cry, run, kick and farm—and farm after they were gone. And that not the first, she prayed. Each of them had been an only child, and children needed children. How she had envied the caravans jammed with children, with dirty-faced boys and girls tumbling out their doors, racing through the encampments, shouting to each other, squabbling, fighting, weeping. And what had he known? Only the memory of a father; and a mother sour with the vinegar of hatred.

If only he had known her condition, how he would have smiled and worried and cossetted her! And made her sit down, and brewed her tea, and asked after her health, and did she have any discomfort? In her misty vision, she could see him coming across the fields with his curly hair wet beneath his cap, his shirt soaked to the skin with sweat, and his mouth and eyes laughing. And she had waited too long.

Now she waited for the priest to arrive to tell her. . . that Paddy was dead. No, not that. But death was in it all, some way, and where was Paddy? Why hadn't he come? She rose from her chair in the sun, conscious of the child within her although as yet there had been no movement. She remembered hearing the tinker women talk about that, about the child kicking them inside.

Father Curtin emerged from the sedan and came slowly up the path toward her, the picture of weariness. Something prompted her to call out.

"He's dead! My Da!"

The priest stopped while Zeke, the collie, sniffed at his feet. He put his left hand to his forehead and then removed his hat. He nodded. "I'm sorry, Jane, to bring you such news."

"And Paddy?"

"Has run off."

She made no answer. The two stood looking at each other across their sorrow.

"He'll not harm himself," Father Curtin said, after a pause. "I imagine he'll be along tonight or tomorrow."

"It had to be," she said. "I don't mean his running off. I mean his killing my Da. He did, didn't he?"

"He did."

She turned and sat down again in the chair she had left beside the door and felt the early chill of the evening.

She would have done anything to undo that strip of the past. She would have given up the child, the farm, her only eye, if only Paddy were back and her father still alive. She had no love for her father, only fear of him, and a sense of duty that seemed to have been built into her bones. She did not mind his death if only it had come some other way—by his own hand, hanged by the police anywhere, shot as a thief, done in by sickness or accident, or dead in a drunken tinker brawl. What made her feel as if her entire inside was a waterfall of tears was the disfigurement of Paddy, the blight he had brought on himself for which he would never forgive himself. She knew him well enough to know that.

She said as much to Father Curtin as he stood with his back to her to hide his own tears, his hand on the collie's head the while, gazing across the field with its stacks of hay.

"He may never come back," she said. "He would die of shame in a jail."

"There's no thought of jail for him," said Father Curtin. "Your father was wanted by the gardai for murder; he killed the shopkeeper in Castle Cove."

"Do they know that?"

"They're satisfied. He was seen."

"Does Paddy know that?"

"I shouted it after him when he fled, and that you were with child." She was sure he was trying to raise her hopes and she stood and stared into his eyes. At length the priest lowered his head.

"I don't think he heard," he said.

She sat down again.

31

NORTH THERE WAS only the sea, gray under the perpetually scudding clouds, striated randomly by the white rage of the waves when the wind was high, undulating ominously in post-storm rancor, rarely blue under the northern sun. About him there was mostly stone, rugged and jagged, leprous white with guano near the nests of the kittiwakes and fulmars, the murres and the few gannets that came north from the Skelligs. Above him in the boggy dell at the center of the island was the only substantial soil and green shrubbery the rocks bore: matted grass, weeds, briar, holly bushes and a small spread of wild flowers on the sheltered slope. No trees relieved the bleak contours.

Six beehive huts, once the cells of austere eremites, remained intact, their corbelled roofs still secure after the slow swing of uncounted centuries, a millennium of defiance of the wild western weather, wind and rain, and rain and the raging winds. The wind was as constant as the lapping, slapping sea and the booming thunder of the surf in the chasms when the ocean rose. Only the irregular counterpoint of the cries of birds—those nesting, those fishing, those migrating—relieved the unrelenting sound of wind and sea. Nature sharpens a man's senses, but it can also harden them to any omnipresent stench or sound. Paddy knew this, but his soul could not shut out the dreadful sounds within his head, the crack and crunch of a skull beneath a bloody boulder.

Walking among the nests for eggs for his survival, he could forget the stink. Sleeping on the dirt floor of a beehive hut he could ignore the cold and the damp. Thorns that scratched him when he picked the few blackberries tangled among the briars went unnoticed, but inside him again and again, like a gong clanging a cacophonous death knell, rose the crack and crunch, and far off the last anguished cry of the priest, meaningless on the wind.

He had been afraid of his mother, afraid of exposing himself to the viciousness of her tongue, afraid of the abuse she heaped on the memory of his father, afraid of the vituperation with which she lashed him, afraid of the indications of the madness that had at last ruined her. He had been afraid because he had had no weapon with which to defend himself, no weapon with which to strike back. Yet he had never thought of running away, of not returning from the fields or from the pub or from mass. He could not go home now, perhaps never again, because he could not face what most in the world he loved and wanted. He was Jane's father's murderer. The word burned in his brain, an incubus, a throbbing terror, a sound of sin and horror and hopelessness. The crime that could not be undone.

No one would find him where he was. It had taken more than month to get to the island, travelling like a tinker over the roads, working an occasional day as a farmhand under an assumed name. He had bought a boat and rowed to the island and let the shabby craft splinter amid the jagged rocks and voracious surf on the north side in the cyclical churning of the sea. That sea thundered behind him now as he walked back from the rocky ledge toward the cell and the stone hut that had become his anchorite's home. He had selected a path he could mount where the low bushes bordering it kept him concealed from the crews of the occasional fishing draggers that chugged past.

One day a picnicking party of two men and two women came to the island and he had to lie for two hours in a ditch on the far side, a ditch protected by brambles and briars from encroachment or approach. The rain came and drove the picnickers off and he had emerged at last sodden and sore. He long hesitated to build a fire. He remembered the fire built by her father, from which he had learned the man's whereabouts. He separated his two layers of clothes and managed to keep one set dry, moving around the island in his underwear when the wind was not too sharp. No one else had come ashore in the three months he had been there. The island was too forbidding with no safe landing and there were other islands close by that were pleasant and accessible.

He did not feel that his isolation and deprivation were sufficient punishment for his crime. He chose five stony sites on the island and each day, careful to see he was not observed, moved from one to another, saying on his knees the rosary he had always carried in his pocket. He said only the sorrowful Mysteries based on the life of Christ: the Agony in the Garden, the Crowning with Thorns, the Scourging at the Pillar, the Carrying of the Cross, and Death on the Cross. He prayed that the Blood of Christ would some day obliterate the blood of Ward that was on him. He was prepared in his soul to wait for years, although already after four months—or was it five months—the agony was mounting, a lust to hear her voice. A lust for a sign.

He would gladly have gone back and faced trial and condemnation and jail, but it would mean facing her and that he could not do. In the nights, in the black heart of his hut, he would see her eyes, those mismatched eyes staring at him, and then watch the blue eye fill up with anguish and accusation, while the dead eye, blank and gray, was even more unbearable because it seemed to shut him out forever. One night the association of those eyes, alive in the darkness, had made him spring in a paroxysm of pain only to strike his head against the low roof of the hut and stun himself. He lay in tears for hours until sleep drowned his consciousness and his pain.

Each day began with the search for food. The berries—they were scarce—mushrooms, eggs of the nesting birds, various greens he could not name, some of which made him ill, and fish, taken from birds he frightened away. The uncooked flesh of the fish was so unpalatable that he determined to chance a fire and decided to build one one night inside one of the stone huts. He had matches, long carried in his pocket; he didn't know why since he had never smoked. But he decided to save them until he was in desperation. For now, he worked at a primitive method of starting a fire. He stored dry grasses and brambles in the hut he had selected for the fire, one not far from his own. He spent hours knocking sparks from stones onto the dried grasses to draw flame, until one day his arms were so weakened they trembled for an hour afterwards. He experimented with diferent types of stone until he found those that most readily produced sparks.

Although he planned to build a fire only at night, the

first time the grasses caught he couldn't restrain himself, heaping more and more grass and dried brambles on the flame and at last a little turf dried from the bog. The fire blazed up and the smoke at first drove him out of the hut, but he had chosen one with an irregular aperture in the roof where a stone had fallen loose and which, as he had hoped, finally and efficiently acted as a chimney. What smoke emerged was swept by the wind and dissipated in the fog and mist.

He ran to his sleeping quarter to bring back a fish he had stolen earlier, and with his pointed stick cooked it over the fire. As he ate, his eyes filled with tears from the smoke of the fire—but also from the memory of his warm kitchen, the stove and the meals she had prepared, and the joy of their mutual affection at the table. But he steeled his mind against the phantoms that plagued him, and settled down to finding the best way to keep some embers in the turf reddened through the day so that in the night he could have his fire.

His daily routine became, if not a comfort, at least a distraction. The foraging for food in the morning, the round of the rosary, the fishing which he finally managed with jetsam found on the rocks, the constant search for debris, the collecting of birds' eggs, the solving of the problem of water. The island was damp, the rain regular, but he had no vessels to collect it, nothing to drink from except his cupped hands. One day two plastic jugs floated in on the tide. He had to swim out to get them and the water was paralyzingly cold. Rinsed out, they proved ideal. He cut them in half with his pocket knife. The bottom parts he used to collect and hold rain water, and the top parts with the caps on them, tipped upside down, served as cups to drink from, complete with handles.

The chief comfort of the daily rounds was the rosary, the regular progress from one stone site to another; a meditation on the sufferings of Christ and the soft oral repetition of the Our Father followed by ten Hail Marys had a hypnotic effect. He had knelt until his knees bled and healed. He was unable not to meditate again and again on his crime, the hideousness of his action, the foolishness of his vengeance, his unfitness before God and before his wife.

He knew his appearance was changing. Only his boots remained whole. Trousers, shirt and jacket became ragged from constant use and from the briars of the few blackberry bushes guarding the entrance to his hiding place against intrusion. The toes and heels of his socks were pretty much gone. He bathed in the sea and washed his underwear in the salt water. He had no mirror to see himself, but he could feel his hair down to his shoulders and his beard down over the open collar of his shirt. He knew that he was losing weight. Yet his mind could rarely dwell on such particulars; always his thoughts were centered on the irretrievability of time. Twice he lost the fire, but the taste of raw fish drove him both times to start it anew using his precious matches. He felt that he was keeping more than the fire alive.

32

THE EARLY REGULAR customers in the Long Bar dealt with all the news in their usual laconic manner. For a brief while the speculation flourished amid a minority of the young that Paddy Madigan had killed the shopkeeper in Waterville as well as Mike Ward. The more mature dismissed the thought and the newspapers soon confirmed their verdict. The newspapers reported that Paddy was wanted by the gardai merely to give a deposition on the circumstances under which Ward had died, careful to avoid any libelous insinuation. The story averred that Paddy would oblige within a day or two.

Father Curtin had told the officers of the Special Branch that he had seen the two men struggling on the ground and that it was a fair deduction that Paddy had killed Ward in self-defense. Ward was his father-in-law and had abused his daughter, to be sure; but also he was wanted for questioning in the Waterville case, was more than likely the murderer there, and was also wanted for questioning in the almost forgotten burglary of Casey's home.

The funeral mass for Ward was offered by the curate.

Jane was the lone mourner, although present in the dark varnished pews were four women and two men, one of them daft, who attended every mass that was offered in Sneem, a nearby summer chapel, and, if she could get transportation, every mass offered in Castle Cove.

Jane insisted that her father be buried on the Madigan farm, that the grave be unmarked and that she not be told the location. She would have had his body cremated (she hadn't known the word), but Father Curtin had told her the Church did not approve of it in Ireland. "We could throw the ashes into the sea," she said, and than added, "It heals all."

Father Curtin attended to the burial. He and the curate dug the grave. The town wasn't told, and in the kitchens of the countryside as well as in the pubs, and the little shops, the final resting place of Mike Ward was never part of the speculation. The main themes were too alluring. The most arresting observations were made at Casey's, for that pub seemed central to the story because of the theft from the Casey household.

"Faith, you never knew for certain that Ward was your man there, did you now?" asked a graybearded gaffer.

"Ah, it was him all right," said Casey. "We're well rid of him."

"Paddy did us all a good turn."

"He did that."

"Ward was a bloody blackguard."

"He used to beat the girl unmerciful, he did."

"There's no luck in a tinker marriage."

"You mean taking a tinker on. By God, there was Deirdre Moriarty down in Blackwater, but in London during the war and she meets this young bucko in uniform, handsome devil, and they marry. He doesn't tell her he's a tinker, didn't have the broad face, ye know. But she finds out when she gets home and he soon has her begging on the streets. It's the tinker way. And didn't the canon tell her it was no grounds for an annulment. She's with him still."

"Ach, it's no life at all, at all."

"I heard of that case."

"Can't you do them the favor of calling them itinerants? It's what the Dail is asking you to do."

"What does it matter what you call them? The bad luck is there."

"Nonsense," came a voice from one of the tables.

"Listen, me boyo. There's Nugent down in Kenmare married a tinker, an itinerant, one of the traveling people, if you will, if that's what you want, and in three months time, the well soured, a fire nearly got the barn, and the cattle were taken with hoosh."

"Hoosh, was it? I heard the sorry story somewhat different."

"Hoosh it was, and hoosh it still is, if I'm any judge of the meaning of the coughs that I heard from them cows."

"And so you think the curse was brought to Paddy?"

"By god, will you read the facts? His mother goes crazy and is down at St. Finian's; the old man comes back and beats the girl again, from what we hear; Paddy goes out and kills him. If that isn't bad luck, what is it?"

A half dozen heads nodded. "I ain't giving Paddy any bad marks for that. He got a killer. Dead of alive, the posters used to say. What?" Casey mopped the bar and quieted the talkers with a flashing eye.

"I'm going to say this before you all, and it's I who ordered her out of here when first she came to town. I say Paddy's got a good woman there, and if there was any curse that went with her it died when Mike Ward died."

It was a week later, after another round of speculation had begun and rehearsed the known material one more time, that a young tow-headed farmer spoke up.

"Where in Christ's name is he? It's been four months now. Or better."

Casey, who ordinarily chided customers for the use of profanity at his bar, folded his arms and said nothing. He refilled the glasses of two huge men who were standing in the twisting lights of the juke box.

"The States!" One of the two nodded sagely.

"Do you know that?"

The man sipped from his stout, wiped his lips on his cuff, and waved an arm dramatically before answering.

"He thinks the law's after him and would catch him in England."

"Why not Australia in that case?" It was the graybeard that spoke. The big man looked at him steadily for a moment and then replied.

"Could be. Could be." He returned to his drink. It was clear he had no information, but the rumor began that Paddy was in Australia.

Father Curtin heard all the speculation, and much that others did not, but it didn't help. He noticed that in all the gossip, discussion and speculation, no one blamed Paddy. Some would have given him a reward, or at least a thank-you.

Paddy hadn't gone to the States. The priest had checked the passport office, even though his instincts told him it wasn't necessary. Dwelling on that scene of horror in Staigue Fort during his daily prayers, and striving on his knees to empathize with the man he knew better than anyone else in town, he arrived at the conviction that Paddy was punishing himself for his crime. At length, all other possibilities were pushed aside.

Motoring one day to Waterville along the coastal road, he saw the Skelligs standing clear on the horizon, sentinels of stone against the sky, jagged bare peaks of a drowned mountain on which for centuries monks had lived in penitential fervor. Seeing those isolated rocks, he knew where Paddy was: in self-imposed exile on an Irish island. Which one? Where?

How slowly the process of reasoning worked. The conclusion when arrived at seemed so obvious that he chided himself for not having thought of it immediately. He had given the problem more time than common sense would justify. The parish duties had seemed to intensify with each passing year, and the slow dissolution of past moral standards in the encroachment of industrialization created new problems. And, yet, fanaticism was long-lived. Did Paddy think he was punishing only himself?

He had had to get hired hands to help Jane on the farm, and in doing so had annoyed Mulcahy, his worthy friend, who had trouble enough with his invalid wife, and short time to find workmen. When her death came at last, Mulcahy's annoyance with him disappeared in the sorrow they shared at the loss of the generous woman, and in the comfort of the church's final rituals.

But Paddy's problem never left Father Curtin's mind—or rather the problem of Paddy. All through the dying months of the year, he felt a burden of responsibility in the matter that his confidence in the goodness of Jane and Paddy never allowed to turn to a sense of guilt.

Dr. O'Brien kept him informed of gossip in the town he

might not otherwise have heard. "They blame you, of course, for having interfered," she told him one afternoon. "'Ah, he shoulda kept his meddling hand out of their lives.' You've heard that, haven't you?"

"Only in my own heart," he replied, removing his eyeglasses and pinching the bridge of his nose between his thumb and forefinger. "So, of course, I knew it was there. With some of them, criticism of the clergy is the only spice in their conversation."

They sat in silence for a full minute, surrounded by the clinical sterilities of her office.

"When is the child due?"

"Before two months have run, for sure."

"Oh, Lord," he said, "have five months passed since Paddy fled? How is she?"

"Healthy as a Mullingar heifer."

"Will you take her to Kenmare?"

"I will not. She won't allow it. She wants the child birthed at the farm in the room, she says, where Paddy was born. And I won't handle the delivery."

"Mrs. McCann?"

"Of course," she said, laughing. "And why not? She has had far more experience than I. As a matter of fact, she's going out there tonight to stay for these last weeks. I'll wait for a call if there's need."

"There's a telephone?"

"There is. Didn't you know? This very week; they come hard. Jane insisted on one, hoping he may call. And Mrs. Sullivan's been very attentive. She's a great help."

He said nothing to her about the conviction he had come to that Paddy had isolated himself on an island in reparation for his sin. He left the office to plan his search, shaking his bowed head at the stupidity that had muddled his vision for half a year.

33

BECAUSE HIS CURATE counseled him that he was letting his concern for Paddy and Jane become too much of an obsession, Father Curtin began his planned search almost furtively. He purchased a book on the islands of Ireland and conned it studiously. He talked with the author on the telephone to find what islands might not be of sufficient interest to be included. In the end, he took the obvious course by starting with the most obvious islands. Garnisch Island to the south, a tropical garden in effect, was too well cared for and too frequently visited to harbor a fugitive.

Local fishermen, eager to help, took him out to the Blaskets, large and once populated but now deserted. Naturalists, residents on the shore, fishermen and his intuition told him that Paddy would not be there. He began moving north into the Galway region and on to Connemara, but his parochial duties called him back and finally, reconciled to facing the critical attention of his curate, he took the younger man into his confidence.

"I am now quite convinced that Paddy is on one of the

smaller western islands," he said, "punishing himself for his crime."

Father Holland was obviously concealing a certain exasperation.

"I can sympathize with you, Father," he said. "You brought the young people together, and you want to reunite them. Now it seems to me that the two major probabilities are what we must consider. It may well be that Paddy does not want to come back and never will come back. Do we not have enough understanding of human nature from the confessional to make us realize that Paddy—and God knows I make no moral judgment—may well have wanted to be rid of marriage anyway, it having driven him to murder? And so, he goes to put it all behind him forever and make a new life elsewhere, leaving Mrs. Madigan, if I may say so, pretty well fixed financially. Father, she has the farm and a small fortune."

Father Curtin looked squarely and thoughtfully at his curate. The young man had enthusiasm, he had sense, he had a profound vocation for the priesthood, but he also had a desire for swift solutions and blunt forthright answers to difficult problems; and, it had to be acknowledged, the fortitude to bear whatever burdens might result from his impetuousness.

"You have assessed the situation admirably," Father Curtin said slowly, "and you are quite right that hours spent in the confessional and in counselling should give us precious insight into human nature. And that's where you fail to understand my relation to Paddy. I was not only his confessor; I was his counsellor. I know him and I understand him, and I love him. He was happy in his marriage; wherever he is, he aches to come back. But his remorse is binding him as surely as a set of manacles."

Father Holland looked thoughtfully at the ceiling. "He's punishing himself?"

"Precisely. When Christ said his yoke was light, He meant just that. The Church doesn't impose penalties on people; it stops people from imposing dreadful penalties on themselves. That's the point of the confessional: you are forgiven, you are given a token penance, you look to the particular judgment and the mercy of God, all dependent on yourself and your sense of contrition. I want Paddy to stop killing himself with insane mortification and remorse and come back to his wife."

It was then that Father Holland agreed to carry on the search and to leave Father Curtin to carry on the parish work. He took off the next day and promised himself a week before he telephoned—unless, of course the unlikely happened and Paddy was found before that. Both agreed that Paddy would not return of his own volition.

"It's not in the man, I'm afraid," Father Curtin said.

Waiting to hear from Father Holland gave Father Curtin some of his most trying days. He told Jane nothing of his conviction that Paddy was in self-exile, like an ancient Irish monk, on some distant island. He would have been long in explaining to her how Irish monks for centuries endured the most austere, self-imposed mortifications, not merely in repentance for their own sins but also for the sins of the world; how the soft Benedictine rule never seemed to suit the Irish; and how the strictures of the East appealed to the Celtic nature more than the moderation of Italy. It was something in the climate. Once one got outside the wine belt, everything grew harsher. No wonder the whole north of Europe became Protestant. No wonder Prussia became the scourge of the continent. Insufficient sunlight had a direct connection with lunacy, he was convinced. Why were people so insistent on being harder on themselves than Holy Mother Church ever could be, or wanted them to be? In our rise from barbarism, the terrible strictures of the past had become the fanaticism of the present.

Two weeks passed, patiently endured, and then two more. Jane's accouchement was at hand. How the priest yearned to have Paddy back at her side for it. And then came light, hope, information. Father Holland telephoned that he had found the island where, he was sure—having circled it and scrutinized it from a boat, and made numerous inquiries—Paddy must be hiding.

"I made no attempt to land," he said, his voice almost lost in the crackling on the line, "much as I would have liked to. It's all yours."

34

FATHER CURTIN'S COMING to the island was exasperating in its details only because of his eagerness to get there. More than six months had passed since Paddy had fled Staigue Fort leaving the corpse of Mike Ward behind him, months in which the priest had himself suffered watching the suffering of Jane, and reflecting on the suffering Paddy had to be enduring.

He had no assurance that Paddy was alive, and he was quite prepared for the dreadful alternative. He had hopes he might bring the tormented man back to his wife so that he might then be at her side when the child was born. He knew it was possible that Paddy, if he managed to find him, might refuse to come. In that case he would appeal to the gardai, who had all but closed the case. He also saw the possibility that he might find a madman, one fit only for confinement. Paddy was, after all, his mother's son, and six months of isolation and exile that indicated fanaticism could induce insanity.

Then again, there was the possibility that Paddy would

not be there, that all the evidence merely shielded an illusion. But Father Holland had been thorough. He had combed the coastline, talking with fishermen, naturalists, yachtsmen and members of the gardai. He had scrutinized half a dozen islands from the decks of draggers, night and day, rain and shine, with powerful binoculars, the patience of Job and a dedication that his superior marveled at. The island he settled on as Paddy's was Inishark, a not uncommon name, which long ago had harbored a small group of monastic ascetics but was never otherwise inhabited, far off the Connacht coast, forgotten by historians and ignored by naturalists, whipped by winds and now little more than a refuge for birds.

Fishermen reported having seen a phantom figure on the rocks, a wraith of gray in the gray morning mists that enveloped the island. Others said they had seen a flame at night, or a hint of flame, that was dismissed as friar's lantern, which seemed to be the local name for ignis fatuus. Three days of study, watching the island through his binoculars from the deck of a boat until his eyes watered from the strain, had rewarded Father Holland at last with a glimpse of a man on his knees half hidden by bushes.

"I would have gone ashore if you had left it to me," he told his pastor.

"No," responded Father Curtin, "thank you. It is so delicate. I have to do it. I know what I am to do."

He went out in a cabin cruiser owned by a classmate from University College, Galway, Rene Kennedy, a fish merchant, who, pledged to secrecy and fascinated by the mystery of it all, was most cooperative. Fortunately, from his youth, Kennedy knew the topography of all the islands including Inishark.

"It's a wonder to me, Dan," he said, "that no youngsters

have been out there and seen the man. When I was tyke I was all over these islands. The present generation, eh, Dan, they're a different breed."

Their first trip to the island proved futile. The surge of the surf prevented the cruiser from getting in close enough for Father Curtin to jump ashore. The second day the sea was calm, but nevertheless they brought a small inflatable rubber dinghy in which if necessary he could row to the island and even abandon it there. He was prepared to swim back to the boat if he had to. What he wanted to take with him for sure was a surplice and a stole. He put both in a waterproof envelope.

They made it neatly. He leaped from the deck to a flat ledge, his borrowed yachting shoes gripping the damp stone's smooth surface reassuringly. He waved to Kennedy to draw the cruiser back from the landing site. He was not intent on surprise. He wanted to be seen. Slowly he climbed the steep jagged incline to the verdant elevation at the heart of the island. One after another he examined the rounded small stone huts, the dilapidated ones as well as those that seemed divinely preserved. Two of them told him what he wanted to know, confirming the judgment of Father Holland. He had put his hand near the turf embers in one of the huts and found them warm. In the other, he found the rude sleeping quarters of the penitent.

Standing before the hut and putting the stole about his neck, he called out:

"Paddy Madigan! Paddy Madigan! She wants you home!"

He paused and cried out again: "I absolve you from your sins in the name of the Father and of the Son and of the Holy Spirit."

No echo came. His words fell into the swirl of sound that came from the sea and the birds. A curlew, far from shore, flew over his head calling, and he thought he had never before sensed the full melancholy of that birds's cry. He turned and walked to the edge of the northern end of the island and called out over the nesting birds, lest a cave below him in the rocks conceal Paddy.

"Paddy Madigan! This is Father Curtin. Jane wants you home. I am absolving you from your sins and from the temporal punishment due to sin. You are free to come home."

He made his way back to the dell and there shouted again.

"Paddy! Paddy! This is Father Curtin. Jane is with child and wants you home. I am absolving you from your sins. Listen to the words of Holy Mother Church. By the power given her by Jesus Christ, the Son of God, and entrusted to me, I absolve you from your sins. You have done your penance."

Once again, at another distant point, the booming of the surf a diapason beneath his words, he called out to the exile. Once he thought he heard one of his words called back to him, but he knew it was an illusion. The very nature of the island induced hallucination.

No answer came, no echo, no hint of a reply. He walked slowly back to the hut with the warm ashes and then to the hut where Paddy had slept. He paused in thought and then, taking off the stole from his shoulder, he stretched its purple length on the gray stone roof of the hut. Turning away, he went to the ledge and found that the surge of surf had risen and that he might have to swim back to the boat. He got ready to do so.

From the deck of the cruiser, Kennedy waved frantically

for him not to swim and began to inflate a rubber raft. One line was flung to the priest and the other cleated to the ship's deck. Dry but sodden with disappointment, he hauled himself back to the cruiser, climbed the ladder, and, wearied by his experience, stood watching the island diminish as they reached for the mainland.

35

THE HEIR TO the Madigan farmlands was born without the father standing by.

Jane had worked in the fields all during her pregnancy, sometimes in the rain that mingled with her tears. She took her stand far from the two farmhands that Mulcahy and Sullivan had hired for her and supervised. She did not want them or anyone to see her tears, and when she faced visitors there were none in her eyes.

The pace of her work slowed greatly toward the end and she confined herself more and more to the house and the kitchen. She had come to fear that Paddy would never return, but refused to acknowledge the fear; she didn't dare dwell on the future. The finality of death, a voice within her kept repeating, can only be followed by other finalities, a finality of flight, a finality of innumerable separations.

The nights became at first intolerable, then for a space tolerable, and then torture. When her father had been alive and a terror for her, she had luxuriated in every solitary hour she could manage in the caravan or at a fireside on the road.

Even the hours spent begging had been quietly endurable. But this new loneliness was something she had never known, nor had dreamed could touch her.

When Paddy had been beside her the evenings had been paradise, especially when she was reading to him and he was listening quietly and on occasion correcting her. She dreamed of those evenings now and she thought of themselves as in a boat sailing above the landscape of Ireland, the rambling shoreline, the green hills and valleys and the idle sheep, the lakes and rivers, the little towns, the mountains, the white-washed country houses, the ruined castles, and the black winding roads with the colorful tinker caravans moving along them, meandering through time.

The child bucking within her brought her out of her reverie. The joy of conception had slowly diminished to a contentment, and then to a satisfaction, and now to a desultory diffidence. She had moments of fright when she thought she might die before he returned and pictured him coming into an empty house. In the moments she thought of him dead, she prayed to die and join him. She moaned at the thought of being left alone with the child and the farm, a situation that loomed as unmanageable for her and thus depressing in the extreme.

She could not forever be dependent on Father Curtin, Mr. Mulcahy and the Sullivans. Kind as everybody had been she had always been uneasy going into town. That had been so even when she went in with Paddy. She could barely endure it now that he was gone. She might have braved it alone gaily if she knew he was at the farmhouse awaiting her return. She arranged to have all her groceries and other supplies delivered to the farm.

As her condition made her reduce the amount of work

in the fields, and as the housework bored her—there was so little of it—she took to walking the boreen at night, as she and he had done together, and where he had so often kissed her. She took a cane with her, lest she fall in the darkness of a moonless night and she kept, Zeke, the collie, beside her.

She welcomed the visits of Dr. O'Brien, whose calls were made more out of friendship and pity than medical necessity. The two talked for hours about the ordeal of delivery and the care of the baby. Eithne Sullivan, her neighbor, was kindness personified, and had talked to her about her own pregnancies.

It was no surprise to her than a midwife would attend her; she never thought of a hospital and a doctor, and had rejected he idea of a hospital when it was proposed. She welcomed the arrival of Mrs. McCann, who came to stay with her as her hour approached.

The woman's presence and personality saved her from collapse. One night after another, in the torment of loneliness, she had sobbed uncontrollably, her tinker stoicism drained entirely. The first night that Mrs. McCann arrived the sobbing had started, and the elderly woman had taken her head in her arms and pressed it gently against the broad gingham expanse of her breasts. Suddenly Jane felt about her a cloud of peace such as she had not known since Paddy left. Vivid images of her own mother came back into her mind. The warmth of affection, the reassuring voice, the cool hands, brought a profound unconscious pleasure to her in being alive and loved. The thought came to her that for the first time in months, she wanted to talk.

"I keep telling myself he'll come back," she said, "and then I keep telling myself he never will. It's like two voices inside me."

She sat with her palms open on her swollen belly feeling

the life inside, shifting occasionally for comfort and watching Mrs. McCann move efficiently about the kitchen, making her tea and neat sandwiches with the crusts cut away such as she had never seen before.

"I've been lonely," she continued. "I thought I was used to being lonely but I wasn't. I didn't know what lonely was." She pushed her left hand across her brow and the bulge of her auburn hair. "I was so happy with him. He was so happy here, but I knew—oh, I knew he would be after my Da. After my Da burned me and Paddy cut me down he changed. He was quieter and he didn't smile as much, and every night I would see him standing and watching the hills. I shoulda known. I shoulda known. But I didn't think. Why didn't I think and tell him?"

"Don't fret, girl, all things happen for the best."

"Paddy is so gentle. I watched him with the sheep and the sick cows."

She looked up at Mrs. McCann, who was now sitting opposite her. How she admired the neat hair and the tidy dress and how she welcomed the pleasant face, and all the kindnesses that she read in it. There was no woman she knew intimately. Her mother had been with her only a short time, and Jane was not yet a woman then. Other tinker women were kind to her, but they were never close; she had had no one in whom she could confide.

The woman who had shown her the most kindness, who had come the closest, was Dr. O'Brien, but there was no maternal affection and always a sense of professional detachment. Mrs. Madigan had been hateful and terrifying and then mad. Now, suddenly and unexpectedly, Mrs. McCann, whom she had first met in Dr. O'Brien's office, who had, indeed, supervised her first bath in a gleaming enamel tub, became for her someone in whom she could confide, who offered all the maternal warmth she had so long been denied.

All sense of estrangement in her melted, and putting down her tea cup and rising from the table, she knelt beside the seated woman and, laying her head in her lap, wept, not the pathetic sobbing of the past, but tears of release.

"Oh, ma'am," she whispered, gazing up at the woman's face, "don't ever leave me."

They were together six days before the baby came. When the pain began, Mrs. McCann put her in the bed where the baby had been conceived and telephoned to Dr. O'Brien.

"Dilatory little brat," said Dr. O'Brien over the telephone, laughing. Mrs. McCann repeated the message to Jane, who didn't know the word "dilatory." But when it was explained to her she laughed too, and repeated the phrase.

It went out of her mind when the contractions intensified, and shortly before the doctor arrived there was a rush of water that frightened her. But remembering Dr. O'Brien's lecture to her on the entire sequence and the various possibilities, she felt easier.

When the doctor came into the room cheerily, she smiled again, but almost immediately had to clench her teeth and reach out wildly with her right hand to grip something. Then Dr. O'Brien gave her something that muted the pain.

"Push, breathe, push, breathe." The commands thundered upon her and then suddenly there was a sense of physical release and the pain was gone and only a soreness remained and Mrs. McCann was holding an infant in the air. Jane closed her eyes and said slowly to herself the prayer the end of which Paddy had taught her and then the baby was put against her breast.

Feeling herself in a daze and not knowing why she

spoke, she asked, "Has Paddy come?"

No answer came, and she recollected that it was a foolish question. The baby cried and Jane began her new life. She resolved to call the child Patrick and wondered how she knew it was a boy. Had someone spoken? Deep within her, she knew that the choice of the name had been made because of an instinctive conviction that Paddy would never return.

36

FATHER CURTIN WENT to the gardai with the information on Paddy's location, the name of the island, the jurisdiction under which it fell, and the necessity for bringing Paddy home. The gardai were most sympathetic. Sergeant Callaghan, who had been through much of it, told him to consult the Special Branch that early on had come down to take charge of the case.

"That case has been referred back to the local Garda Síochána," an officer said. "It's their problem now. Didn't I understand it was all cleared up down there?"

Up, down—no one knew where the case stood or seemed to care. Sergeant Callaghan was surprised to hear that the case had reverted to him. It was a responsibility he did not want. Unlike many ambitious officers, he did not resent the intrusion of the Special Branch. He would check with the Special Branch. Unable to make headway on the telephone, he conducted his inquiry my mail, keeping Father Curtin informed on each step of the process.

"Can't you ask the gardai in Connemara, at Clifden, say, to go out to the island and bring the man in?" the priest asked.

Sergeant Callaghan didn't think so. The next week he thought so, and messages went back and forth over the wires. A week later the gardai in Clifden reported to Sergeant Callaghan that they had checked the island and, while there was evidence of picnickers having had a fire in one of the stone huts, they found no one living on the island, and, having the details of the case related to them by the Special Branch, saw no reason for wasting their time checking barren islands for a man no one really wanted.

"Father," Sergeant Callaghan said, twirling his large mustache between thumb and forefinger, "you can see the problem. All right, Paddy is a missing person, but he's not wanted for any crime. There's a reward for capturing Mike Ward waiting for Paddy. All we want from Paddy is a deposition. Ward? I'd have killed him myself if I could have laid hands on him, or they gave me a revolver I've been requesting for years."

A second appeal to the Clifden patrol sent another searching party to the island with no result .

"Father," Sergeant Callaghan relayed, "they say they haven't time to be playing games on the islands with eccentrics. It might be different if there was a murder charge against the fellow, they say. Is he dangerous, they ask? No, says I. Then, says they, go after him yourself."

Father Curtin took the matter up again with Father Holland, who, he could see, was most eager to be off to the hurling match and not again be discussing the Madigan file, as the mystery story writers labeled such affairs.

"I see only one way. I must bring the woman and the child to the island and let them stay until he sees them."

Father Holland agreed all too hastily and hurried out of the room. Father Curtin walked wearily to the library and took up the London *Times* and *Le Figaro*, for he always found comfort and distraction in reading French. But he could not concentrate. He threw down the papers and turned to the telephone to call Rene Kennedy in Moyard, outside Clifden.

In his inner vision, the smashed bloody face of the tinker lying in the grass of Staigue Fort stared up at him, and the single blue eye was mocking him: evil breeds evil, and the stoutest ally of evil is apathy.

Kennedy's voice from Moyard as it came crackling over the wire drove the vision of the dead tinker out of his head.

"Dan," said Kennedy, "let's have another crack at that island. We'll both go ashore and root him out."

"Thanks, Rene, we will. But I have a plan that will lure him out of hiding if anything will." His determination was firm.

37

WHEN PADDY HEARD at long last the engine throbs of the cabin cruiser as it withdrew from the island that day, he rose achingly from the ditch where he had lain hidden, submerged in leaves, half underground. He crawled along the tunnel he had cut through the briars until he could stand erect on the matted grass beside the wild holly, uncertain as to what he had heard, more than half unbelieving.

Mists were massing at the northwestern end of the island and he rubbed his eyes, afraid that he would have still another illusion. He feared that he might be growing deranged. In his head he had been suffering pains that on occasion blinded him, and other pains in his chest and left arm with its badly healed fist, pains that left him gasping in agony. He had to rest more often than before, and he suffered fits of weakness that left him unable to move for hours. The thought of losing his mind was the one thing that would have made him leave the island—and he had not faced the alternative. The figures in the mist were only mist—and yet, someone might have stayed on the island, someone might be waiting. If he heard a voice, he knew whose voice it would be.

He half hoped that what he heard was an illusion, a dream, brought on by his mental and now physical pain, by his months of mortification. He had seen the boat approaching, obviously headed for the island, and without waiting to see what manner of man might be aboard he fled to his hiding place from which he could see nothing and, covered with leaves and sods, could hear little. He was invisible even to someone who might stand over him and no one would ever walk to the spot.

The ditch had seemed colder and his limbs wearier. He hated the intrusion. No one had come since picnickers months ago. Boats had circled the island, but not attempted a landing. Bird watchers, perhaps, but other islands offered them more. Was this someone coming for him? The gardai at last? He felt that they wouldn't bother over the death of Ward—and yet it was murder and the law might force them.

He thought he heard a footstep on the loose stones of the path to the beehive huts and then silence, and then a voice wrapped in wind calling his name, and words that he could not catch. A short while later, from another quarter, the voice again, the words lost in the screeching swirl of the birds, roused from their nests by the intruder. Again he heard the voice at a distance, shouting, and he thought he recognized it as that of Father Curtin. He almost rose to rush out, but then he slumped back, knowing he could face neither the priest nor the police, least of all Jane because of the wound he had inflicted on her. He had debated the matter in his mind but was afraid to think what she might say. His mind ached with the dilemma until, quite near him, he heard the priest's voice ring out, every word a clarion.

"Paddy Madigan, this is Father Curtin! Jane wants you

home! She is with child! I am absolving you of your sin and any temporal punishment due to sin; you have done your penance; your sin is washed away. Listen to the words of Holy Mother Church by the power given her by Jesus Christ, the son of God. *Absolvo te.* I absolve you of your sins, in the name of the Father and of the Son and of the Holy Spirit."

Paddy sobbed in the ditch and started to crawl out, but again a half-understood psychological force held him back. He waited until, half risen, he could hear the diminishing throb of the engine, which told him that the temptation was beyond recall. He walked boldly to the edge of the island to watch the departing boat. He had been discovered.

He dared not leave the island; he could not leave the island; he was afraid to leave the island.

He returned to his hut repeating the priest's words. It was no illusion. Jane was with child. It couldn't be. A trick? He fell on his knees, with his head against the rocks of the hut.

He would wait for a sign.

38

A WEEK PASSED painfully, spent in arranging the detailed logistics. At last, they motored to Connemara, Father Curtin, Dr. O'Brien, Jane and the baby bundled in blue and thriving. The evening of their arrival was spent at the Kennedy home, a white Georgian mansion, elegantly modernized. Rene and his wife Bertha received them with enthusiasm—and for Rene, with the thrill of being part of a conspiracy.

Jane felt terrified at what lay before her, and at the same time ached to get launched on it. The spaciousness of the Kennedy house made a profound impression on her and enabled her to contain herself as she wandered through it, fed the baby and bedded him for the night, and then joined the others for dinner. For her the house held majesty and mystery, and she walked through it as a child might walk through a palace. She had never dined at such a table as was set, and if it had not been for Dr. O'Brien on her right, quietly coaching her with affectionate humor, gently explaining the civilities, she might have fled from the scene.

Everyone was more than kind and she became very

attentive when she was told what she must do on the following day.

"He will come to you where he would go to no one else," Father Curtin said. He explained the pains he had been to on the island to make sure that Paddy had heard that he was forgiven and that his wife wanted him home.

"He will believe it when he sees you," he said. Getting onto the island would be difficult, but Rene Kennedy's two sons, strapping in size, would help her. Kennedy outlined the procedure like a field marshal, going into tedious detail.

As he became repetitious, Jane's mind wandered back to the day Father Curtin had driven down to the farm to tell her that he was convinced that Paddy was alive and that they knew where he was. She had seized his hand and kissed it. He had recounted to her then the details of his trip to the island, and all that he had said and done. She had felt herself sway with inner happiness.

"But he didn't appear," she had said in renewed alarm.

"No. . . I don't know what I expected. . ."

"Then how do you know he is still alive?"

He had told her of the ashes in one hut and the bedding in the other.

"The ashes were warm?"

"They were." He had said it to her a dozen times. From her life on the roads, she had known what that meant.

"Thank God. Thank God!" She had kissed his hand again and held it to her cheek, but conscious of his slight embarrassment, she had stood upright and told him he had to get her to the island. From that moment, she would hear no delay.

She had run back to the house to tell Mrs. McCann, who had stayed on with her since the birth of the child, and she had hugged the woman and wept in her arms, and said again and again, though mostly in a whisper, "He's alive! He's alive." Mrs. McCann had exulted with her. She had turned from Mrs. McCann's embrace and taken up the child in her arms and held him and told him over and over again that his father was alive and that they were going to him.

Her love of boats made the trip to the island a double pleasure. But as they neared the forbidding outpost a sense of terror seized her.

"Father, father, what will we find?"

"Him," the priest said simply. "Him."

"I'm frightened."

"Trust the Lord, Jane, trust."

He led her to the bow of the boat and stood with her at a point where they might be seen. The landing was difficult, and it took both the young Kennedys and Father Curtin to get her and the child ashore, safe and dry.

"I hope to hell you know what you're doing," Dr. O'Brien said to him grimly.

"Doctor," he said, "I'm sure I understand his mind."

"*Understood* it, you mean—when he was sane!"

They had not meant for Jane to hear such words as she stood upright on the ledge with her son in her arms, but the words carried across the water. She heard. But she was not afraid. She knew that Paddy—if he were on the island, if he were physically able—would show himself to her where he had shrunk from showing himself to Father Curtin. She would see him; he would be well.

"Go to the highest point of the island," Father Curtin had told her, "and stand there with Patrick in your arms. If he doesn't come—then sing. . . sing! Sing as loud as you can, any song at all. Sing from your heart. There is no danger. We will be here below, out of sight, waiting on the rocks."

And so she went up the hill carrying the baby in the crook of her left arm, her right held out to balance her over the uneven stony ground. Her thick auburn hair was caught up with a green ribbon, and the tweed suit she wore had a pepper-and-salt weave with a greenish tint. Dr. O'Brien had selected if for her. But she had insisted on wearing around her shoulders the tinker blanket that he had washed for her.

As she neared the height, her insides turned to jelly and sweat poured from her armpits and her palms. Her mind was turbulent—there was so much that could happen, all the guesswork might be wrong.

At the crest, she paused and stood still, surveying the island around and below her. The beehive huts stood like blackened petrified hay stacks. They looked ominous, but not far from her some brave flowers trembled in the breath of the west wind. For a few seconds, she daydreamed about the farm. Minutes crept by, interminably, marked off by the cries of the kittiwakes, the booming of the surf on the west side of the island, and the squawking of some young bird in the bushes behind her.

She heard a slight and different noise to her right. She began to feel faint. To strengthen herself, she cleared her throat to bring herself to call out or to sing or to say his name. She turned her body so that the face and vision of the child would be in the direction from where the noise came, a noise that was now gathering into a movement. He would see the infant and her face as he came.

She saw him, and she staggered and almost fell. She had dreamed of him as she had seen him last, his black curls and his smile and his broad shoulders. What was coming at her now came as an animal might come, as if on all fours, stooped over and stumbling, disheveled in its rags, the hair hanging low on both sides of his face, and the alien beard obscuring everything but his tortured eyes. The figure that had been so broad was emaciated, and his right hand was grasping the purple stole that seemed like a stripe of blood against his chest.

She was unable to speak but was gasping. Tears poured from her eyes, blinding her. At last she called out his name in anguish, and she saw him fall at her feet as still as the stones on which she was standing.

39

FROM THE YARD of the presbytery, Father Curtin could see the low-slung dark green mountains, darker still where the reforestation marched in a straight line up the slope. His expectation was correct: the caravan was moving slowly down from the ancient pass, its canvas still another shade of green—the forty-first, say, added to Ireland's traditional forty.

He decided it would be best if he drove out to the farm to await them and to welcome their arrival. He changed his clothes, gave himself half an hour, alerted Doctor O'Brien, and with her, at length, drove slowly north, his mind at rest.

"Thank God," he said to her, "you were with us that day at the island."

"Sometimes," she said, "you do things right—though not bloody often." And they both laughed.

"What's your next project?" she asked.

"To get you a husband."

"He's got to have a house like the Kennedys."

He turned the sedan into the boreen leading to the Madigan farm. Three months had passed. The recovery had been slow. Two months were spent in the hospital in Killarney. As Paddy's strength returned, his mother's waned. She died the day he was released, and the funeral was held the next day. When the question of convalescence arose, the doctor recommended a trip, and it was Jane who made the final suggestion.

"I'll take him in a tinker's cart to the ends of the world," she said, her smile broadening. "Sure, it's the life I know best, and what could be better for him than the life of the roads?"

To welcome them home, Father Curtin stood in the farmyard with Dr. O'Brien and Mrs. McCann—and Zeke, the collie, who was obviously aware of a significant event developing.

When Jane saw them, she stood up from the seat at the front of the caravan with the reins in her hands and shouted out a greeting.

"Cead mile failte," the priest responded. "Welcome home!"

She jumped from the seat to the ground and embraced Dr. O'Brien, and then the priest, and then called out to Mrs. McCann, who had returned to the house and was now coming out again. Father Curtin had never seen Jane so elated, so gay, so sure of herself.

"They're both sleeping in back," she said. "Even my shouting didn't wake them. I was going to wake him to see the farm from the hill. It was golden in the sun."

"Let them sleep," Father Curtin said. "They'll wake to a new life."

About the author . . .

HERBERT A. KENNY is a native of Boston and a graduate of Boston College (class of 1934). He was for many years Editor for the Arts and Humanities of *The Boston Globe*, and, more recently, literary columnist of the *Boston Irish Reporter.* He was a member of the governor's committee that formed the Massachusetts Council on the Arts and Humanities and subsequently served as a member of the Council. He was one of the founders of the National Book Critics Circle.

He is a poet, critic and author of fourteen other books, including *Newspaper Row: Journalism in the Pre-Television Era, Literary Dublin: A History,* and *Cape Ann/Cape America* (new paperback edition, 1999). His work has appeared in a variety of publications and anthologies and he is a contributor to the *Catholic Encyclopedia*.

Herbert Kenny lives in Manchester-by-the-Sea, Massachusetts, but over the years he has been a frequent visitor to Ireland, which he has chosen as the setting for his first novel, *Paddy Madigan*.